KEEPER OF THE ALGORITHM

H. Peter Alesso

Novels by
H. Peter Alesso

THE KEEPER SAGA

Keeper of the Algorithm © 2023
Keeper of the Secret © 2023
Keeper of the Truth © 2023

THE HENRY GALLANT SAGA

Midshipman Henry Gallant in Space © 2013
Lieutenant Henry Gallant © 2014
Henry Gallant and the *Warrior* © 2015
Commander Gallant © 2016
Captain Henry Gallant © 2019
Commodore Henry Gallant © 2020
Henry Gallant and the Great Ship © 2020
Rear Admiral Henry Gallant © 2021
Midshipman Henry Gallant
at the Academy © 2022

Other Novels

Captain Hawkins © 2016
Dark Genius © 2017
Youngblood © 2018

Short Story Collection

All Androids Lie © 2022

KEEPER OF THE ALGORITHM

H. Peter Alesso
hpeteralesso.com

© 2023 H. Peter Alesso

This is a work of fiction. All
characters, dialog, and events
portrayed in this book are fictional,
and any resemblance
to real people or incidents is purely coincidental.

All rights reserved.

No part of this publication may
be reproduced, stored in
a retrieval system, or transmitted
in any form or by any
means without prior permission in writing from

VSL Publications
Pleasanton, CA 94566

ISBN-13
Edition 1.00

∞

Deus ex Machina

versus

Diabolus ex Machina

SYNOPSIS

Once a misfit dropout, Mike now controls the fate of man versus machine

In a world where the boundaries between man and machine blur, your thoughts, emotions, and yearnings are no longer private. The confluence of biotech and infotech has given birth to the Algorithm—a force that predicts your every move and has the power to shape your deepest desire.

But when the Algorithm starts undermining human worth, many find themselves obsolete. Grappling with their waning relevance, they find solace in a new realm. They master the skills of a surreal virtual world that requires neither gravity nor light.

As technology's grip tightens, a haunting question emerges: Does anyone hold the reins of the omnipotent Algorithm?

Enter an unlikely hero—an aimless dropout who unwittingly finds himself at the nexus of power. Tall and lean, Mike has deep-set hazel eyes that often reflect his internal conflicts and dilemmas. His past is riddled with disappointment and insecurity.

Assuming another student's ID in a crowded exam room, Mike's journey takes an unexpected turn when a stern figure declares, "I am Jacob Winters. Welcome to the AI career placement test. Today, we will discover which of you represents the pinnacle of human genius."

Delve into *Keeper of the Algorithm* to discover a future where destiny is written in code and domination is the ultimate prize.

For serious AI enthusiasts only!

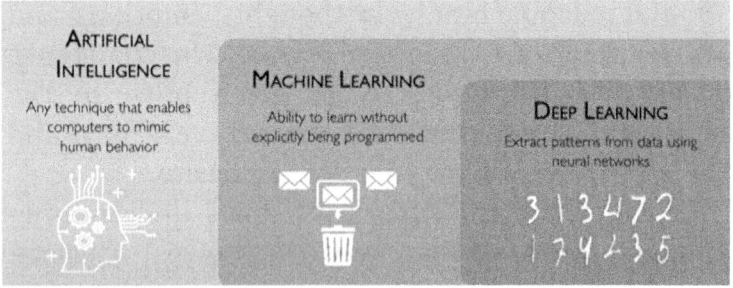

CONTENTS

Chapter 1 Outlier
Chapter 2 Twin
Chapter 3 Keeper
Chapter 4 Guise
Chapter 5 Assignment
Chapter 6 Clear Sailing
Chapter 7 Invisible Hand
Chapter 8 Implementation
Chapter 9 WormAI
Chapter 10 Clueless
Chapter 11 Cha-cha
Chapter 12 Breach
Chapter 13 Deep Dive
Chapter 14 Downhill
Chapter 15 Suspicion
Chapter 16 Covert Ops
Chapter 17 Surgery
Chapter 18 Ex Machina
Chapter 19 Shadows
Chapter 20 Crunch
Chapter 21 Healing
Chapter 22 Money
Chapter 23 Silk Road
Chapter 24 Firewall

Chapter 25 Mole
Chapter 26 Truth
Chapter 27 Enough
Chapter 28 Dangling Ove the Edge
Chapter 29 Diabolus ex Machina
Chapter 30 Dev Con II
Chapter 31 War Games
Chapter 32 Night Out
Chapter 33 Return Fire
Chapter 34 Hammer
Chapter 35 Dynamo
Chapter 36 Only Human
Chapter 37 Winner Takes All
Chapter 38 Bedfellows
Chapter 39 Keeper of the Secret
Chapter 40 Bewildering
From the Author
Coming Soon

CHAPTER 1

Outlier

Mike arrived early on a frosty Saturday morning in April to take an exam using another student's ID, testifying to both his ability and flawed life choices.

He didn't know Michael Stewart, nor did he care why he couldn't take the test. Michael would get his desired 720 score, and Mike would bank his digital payment.

While he didn't like cheating, it was a necessary source of income since he had burned his own career chances last year.

Tall and lean, Mike had deep-set hazel eyes that often reflected his internal thoughts and dilemmas. His hair was long and brown, and a lock often fell across his forehead. His tousled manner highlighted his youthful energy. He wore casual clothes, distinguishing him from the two hundred more polished students taking their seats.

A crisp bell rang.

Ting!

Inside the vast, echoing chamber of the exam room, there was an aura of palpable tension, a sensation of electricity in the air. The walls were adorned with timeworn wooden panels and faded photographs that seemed to tell the stories of past geniuses. Shafts of soft sunlight streamed through tall, arched windows, illuminating motes of dust dancing in the air.

Rows and rows of desks stretched across the room, each holding a prodigy. They sat, statues of concentration. Poised before their computer screens, the weight of their collective intellect pressed on the room.

Mike nervously swiped a lock of hair out of his eyes and sat awkwardly in his chair. His disheveled appearance differed from the room's gravitas. But his bright, eager eyes revealed a deep passion and an unquenchable thirst for knowledge. He could feel over two hundred sets of eyes searching the room —an unspoken competitiveness among them. Each one knew the sacrifices, the late nights, and the insurmountable challenges they had overcome to get here.

There was an almost haunting silence, interrupted only by the occasional shuffle of feet or the barely audible sigh of anxiety. The room's stillness was a testament to the magnitude of the moment— the calm before the storm of mental prowess that was about to be unleashed.

A stern-faced man stood at the front of the room. His voice resonated with a deep timbre, filling every crevice of the cavernous space.

"I am Jacob Winters, and I wish to congratulate you on competing in the Turing Institute's AI Career Placement Examination."

Jacob Winters exuded an aura of power, charisma, and sophistication. His sartorial choices reflected his personality—a sharp, tailored suit paired with a designer tie. In his late forties, he had a chiseled jawline, piercing grey eyes, and dark, immaculately groomed hair combed back. His entire physical demeanor screamed authority. He was acutely aware of the impression he made, using it to his advantage.

He said, "You are the most elite AI talent in the world. The top AI organizations are searching for their next Algorithm Keeper. Microsoft, Amazon, and Anthropoid, among others, have their sights set on you."

Mike felt a rush of adrenaline mixed with anxiety and exhilaration. This was the crucible, the proving ground where futures were forged.

Whispers erupted. "I've got Google in the bag," boasted a voice to Mike's left.

His neighbor quipped, "Start-ups are the future. That's where I'm heading."

Though Mike had taken myriad exams under different identities, the weight of this one felt different. The world's brightest were here, yet he felt an unshakable confidence. After all, he was good at what he did.

Winters resumed, "You have three hours. While you may employ any AI to aid you, I'd advise you to remain consistent. Mixing and matching—Bard, GPT, Llama—might muddy your answers."

Mike planned to use DeepMind IV. It boasted the most recent neural net upgrades.

Winter's final words echoed, "And beware! Your partnership with AI is under scrutiny as much as your prowess."

Mike took a moment and closed his eyes. He allowed memories to cascade through his mind. The image of him being expelled from MIT for cheating emerged. Ironically, he hadn't cheated. A student had approached him in the study hall and asked for help with a few questions. Mike reluctantly obliged. Later, when Mike realized the questions had turned up on the final exam, he said nothing. However, a teacher recognized that the student's answers were similar to Mike's and accused them of cheating.

The other student confessed but said that Mike was the one who stole the test.

Mike was expelled.

That he survived as an undesirable outcast was a testament to his resilience.

A bell interrupted him.

Ting!

Winters said, "You may begin."

Mike felt a smile tug at the corner of his lips.

Game on.

Mike opened the provided laptop and tapped Michael Stewart's ID authentication pin against the touch screen. It automatically signed him in.

The first few questions were easy enough for him to rely on his eidetic memory. But soon, he became hesitant as more complex questions appeared. He put on his AI virtual glasses to meld with DeepMind and buckled down to solve the more intricate problems.

The glasses seamlessly synced with the laptop.

By shifting his eye's focus and blinking, he could select options from the glasses' virtual hologram.

He wanted to get Michael Stewart a top grade to receive his payment. However, he was encountering more difficulty as the test progressed.

He became stuck on one issue for a long time, but slowly, he coaxed DeepMind into developing a reasonable solution. Still, he wasn't sure if it was right.

Over the next half hour, he began picking up speed. He was fascinated by the exam because it was unlike anything he had ever seen before.

Yet he made good progress, restoring his confidence, until he hit a second complication. This question was so weird that he could not recall a single fact relating to solving it, even with his eidetic memory.

Again, he worked feverishly with his AI until a potential solution emerged.

Sighing, he continued.

Unfortunately, he encountered another perplexing problem that addressed extending NP-completeness. He saw failure looming ahead.

This might ruin Stewart's chances and cost me my payment.

He tried multiple methods and procedures, but they all failed. Finally, he had an insight and began a solution, hoping for partial credit. With only seconds left, he took a wild guess and finished.

Mike put his glasses in his pocket. He wanted to leave, knowing that he not only cheated but might have also failed. But before he could move, he noticed security guards entering the room and taking positions around the area.

Winters said, "All students are to remain seated while the exam is scored."

They received their grades, starting with the lowest. Each student touched their ID pin to the computer screen one by one, transferring the score. Their career assignment was included, and they were to report to work the next day.

Soon, all two hundred students stood up and left until Mike was the only one remaining.

Finally, Winters approached Mike and said, "Please come with me."

As they walked, the luxury of the main room gave way to a more intimate corridor. Exquisite art pieces and relics punctuated it. It led them to a small alcove room, starkly contrasting the grandiosity outside. This room, however, had its charm—minimalist yet warm. The walls were a soft shade of cream. The subtle glow of a single table lamp casts a gentle shadow, creating a sense of discreet confidentiality. Despite its comforts, the room seemed charged with urgency and expectation.

Seated at a glass table was a young woman. Her presence contrasted with the room's simplicity. Her poised demeanor showed strength, yet her eyes held a spark of spirit.

"This is my special assistant, Amber Hearst," Winters introduced, his tone hinting at pride. Amber beamed with calm reassurance. The room seemed to brighten. But behind Amber's composure, Mike could sense an underlying tension—a weight of responsibility she bore.

Amber said, "Congratulations, Michael Stewart, your score was five standard deviations from the mean. That makes you a 1 in a billion outlier."

She smiled and offered her hand to congratulate him.

As he shook her hand, Mike squirmed and thought,

The only problem is . . . I'm not Michael Stewart.

Amber explained, "There were three Easter Eggs hidden within the exam. Two were formidable but known challenges. The third one I slipped in as a playful jest while drafting the test. I thought it was an unsolvable enigma, a mere diversion. But you've shattered that assumption."

Winters's stern visage broke into a radiant smile, his eyes twinkling with excitement. "Michael, your talents have impressed us and shown a rare promise. The Turing Institute will undoubtedly benefit from having you on board."

Mike furrowed his brow as he processed the

weight of their words. He looked nervously at the security guard. His voice was barely more than a whisper, "This is . . . overwhelming."

Despite Mike's protests, Amber swiftly initiated an identity verification procedure. The cold scanner grazed his retina, the pads captured the whorls of his palm, and the soft swab brushed his inner cheek. Within moments, the data was synthesized into a Turing Institute ID pin with Michael Stewart's name.

As she replaced Mike's old pin with the new Turing pin, Amber remarked with finality, "Your credentials have been updated into the mainframe. Starting tomorrow, you'll wear a wrist monitor. It will continuously sync your biological information, creating a Digital Twin. It will follow you wherever you go to maintain a record in the government's Human ID Database."

Winters said, "The pin and the monitor will allow you to access every element of the Turing Institute's research for the Algorithm."

As the enormity of the situation began to dawn on him, Mike felt a cold shiver run down his spine. But before he could fully react, Winters' firm handshake pulled him back to reality. "Welcome aboard, Michael. Tomorrow marks the beginning of your new journey."

As Winters departed, Amber lingered, her eyes assessing Mike with curiosity and skepticism. "You might have fooled Winters and the system, but you don't fool me," she said, her voice barely above a whisper.

Mike's heart raced.

Does she know?

She continued, "Your knowledge . . . your abilities . . . it's not just the result of academic study and an eidetic memory. There's something exceptional and unique about you. I've seen it before."

"In a mirror, perhaps?" he guessed.

She smiled. "I'll be watching you as someone who knows what it's like to walk on the edge."

Their dynamic had now changed into a dance of possibility and caution.

As he exited the Institute, Mike thought,

I've outsmarted situations before, but this… have I ensnared myself in an irreversible trap?

The need to hack into the impregnable Human ID Database and erase everything raced through his mind.

That's impossible!

CHAPTER 2

Twin

The door yielded to a gentle push, revealing an apartment awash in soft, dim amber light. The space felt like a realm caught between the old and the new. The high ceilings with ornate moldings whispered of a bygone era while state-of-the-art tech gadgets dotted the room. The walls were adorned with art—some abstract, some hauntingly realistic. Overflowing with a mélange of tomes, bookshelves stood like silent sentinels on either side of the room.

The sounds of a classical piano sonata floated through the air, contrasting with a faint hum and beep from a computer.

As Mike's gaze swept across the room, it landed on Michael Stewart, a silhouette framed before a piano. He was seated in a sleek, modern wheelchair. The metallic sheen was coldly clinical against the warm, textured fabrics of the apartment. The sight was unexpected and disorienting.

Stewart's face showed signs of a tough life, even in the dim light. His deep-set eyes bore into Mike, reflecting perception and perhaps a hint of concern. His lips curled into a faint, welcoming smile, but the softening of the lines on his face revealed a vulnerability.

There was a pause, a heartbeat, and then Mike broke the silence.

"I didn't know," he uttered, his voice laden with genuine surprise and a twinge of guilt.

With a grace that defied his physical constraints, Stewart maneuvered his wheelchair forward. "Many things aren't evident over pixels and text," he responded.

Mike's initial shock began to ebb, replaced by a rising tide of curiosity and compassion.

Stewart's voice conveyed his predicament. "I had a car accident and broke my spine, but I couldn't get proper medical treatment without premium medical insurance. That's why I needed you to take my place and pass the exam with top grades."

Mike took a moment to process. He noticed a red envelope lying on the piano marked 'final notice.' He said, "I see. So, if you secured a job offer, it would grant you the necessary medical coverage. Later, you could fabricate an accident scenario to qualify for the required surgery."

Stewart nodded, a slight grimace betraying the pain of his condition. "That was the idea. But now, seeing you here, unplanned . . . did you not pass the examination?"

Mike hesitated, the weight of their shared deception bearing down on him. "The nature of the exam wasn't what I expected," he murmured, letting the implication hang in the air.

"I was afraid you might not accept the challenge if you knew."

Mike chuckled.

The silence between them was laden with anticipation and fear. Stewart's voice, heated with urgency, pressed again. "So, did you fail?

Taking a deep breath, Mike met Stewart's gaze, "I'm afraid it's not about passing or failing. The situation has become far more complicated than that."

Stewart frowned.

"I passed the test but was assigned a Keeper position at the Turing Institute."

"Wow! You must have blown the top off that exam."

"Unfortunately, I did."

"Why do you say that? Will that keep me from my goal?"

Mike, avoiding a direct answer, asked, "Do you know what a Digital Twin is?"

Stewart raised an eyebrow, intrigued. "Sounds familiar but refresh my memory."

"It's a computer replica of a person," Mike started, gauging Stewart's understanding. "It mirrors one's every move and biological response. With discreet devices as common as a cell phone and wrist monitor, it reflects every heartbeat and step I take."

"Meaning?"

"Starting tomorrow, every move I make will be cataloged as Michael Stewart."

"That's a disaster," said Michael with a frown.

"There's no way I can hack the Human ID Database to erase the situation. We're caught in this trap."

Michael shook his head. "Yesterday, I just wanted to get medical treatment. Now, I want to disappear."

"If you had asked me that yesterday," said Mike, "I would have said that I wanted a second chance for a career. Now, I only want to avoid prison."

"How can we survive this mess?" Stewart's eyes flickered with desperation. "Life, Mike, has always been about blurred lines. Look around," he gestured expansively to the art and tech-filled room. "Art is both truth and imagination. Technology, while it brings us together, also isolates us. It's all a matter of perception."

Mike nodded thoughtfully. "I always hoped that tech could be our way forward. But now, it feels like a noose tightening around our necks."

Stewart looked gloomy.

But Mike stood up, his eyes glinting with determination. "Perhaps it's time to rewrite the game's rules. If technology is a beast . . . then let's tame it."

Stewart asked hopefully, "You have an idea?"

Mike laughed. "Perhaps."

He held up a tiny gleaming device. "With my new Turing ID pin, I may be able to trick the system. Before the twinning starts, I can edit our personal information. By matching my biological data with your educational background, we can merge into the new Michael Stewart."

Stewart sighed, his shoulders slumping. "That makes twins of you and me. But while technology may be duped, human memory can't. How do we mislead those who already know us?"

Mike shrugged. "I don't have much family."

Stewart admitted, "Neither do I. My abusive, alcoholic father deserted us when I was ten. Now, my mother is on the dole, living in a small apartment in Virginia. She did her best for me and helped me get a scholarship to MIT. Things were looking up until the car accident."

"Ha. My life wasn't so different," said Mike. "My mom lives on the dole in the Midwest. I never knew my father. Mom said that was a good thing. I, too, got a scholarship to MIT but was thrown out last year."

Stewart laughed. "It's almost hilarious how we have become twins."

"Yes. Now we are conjoined," Mike chuckled. "I must be 'you' working at Turing, and you must disappear into the background. Only appear for your medical treatment when I've earned enough money to pay for it off the books."

"Okay, but you must move into this apartment with me."

Mike looked around at the art, music, and

technology and liked the idea.

"Yes. We must become roommates to maintain the illusion of the new Michael Stewart's existence."

"Precisely. It's a strategy." With a deep sigh, Stewart voiced the undeniable truth, "Our destinies are now inextricably linked. The Turing Institute's position and perks are our ticket out. We must navigate this together."

Mike reflected, "In this game, the boundaries between real and fabricated are blurred."

CHAPTER 3

Keeper

The sprawling campus of Turing Institute lay in a lush green valley outside of Cambridge, Massachusetts. Mike was breathless as he returned to the main building. He paused inside the open door of Winters' office. The room spoke to practicality and discipline. Yet, the window behind Winters's desk offered an extravagant panoramic view of the landscape's sprawling skyline. Sunlight filtered through, casting geometric shadows on the mahogany flooring

At first glance, the private sanctum of the great leader reminded Mike of a family home office. The space was crammed with intimate personal possessions of Jacob Winters, collected over a lifetime. Memorabilia, trinkets, and photos of his wife and family crowded the shelves. There was a display case of family trophies, ribbons, and awards.

"Come in, come in, Michael," boomed the

commanding voice as he waved Mike to the sofa across from his chair. He wrapped his hands around Mike's hand, pumping it like an affectionate father.

"Glad to see you one-on-one at last. Have a seat. I've reviewed your exam with growing fascination. I said to Amber, 'That boy bears watching.'"

"I . . . I, . . . huh," fumbled Mike, taken aback by the nature of the boisterous welcome.

"How about joining me in a snack?" asked the Keeper of the Algorithm as he tore his sandwich in half.

"It's grilled cheese and ham. My favorite."

"Thank you, sir." Mike took the sandwich and placed it on a plate before him.

"Sorry to ask you to drop by so abruptly, but I never seemed to have a minute to myself anymore. When my morning appointment was unavoidably delayed, I grabbed the opportunity." He took a large swallow of coffee and said, "Ahh, no one makes coffee like my Maria. She prides herself in brewing it special for me."

Mike blinked as he recalled that Maria was the Keeper's wife. He glanced around and noticed a photo of an attractive woman with a pleasant smile atop the large desk. The sadness in her eyes hinted at the uneasy bargain she had made as the lonely wife of a dedicated professional.

The shift in Mike's gaze didn't escape Winters, a shadow crossed his features. "Life demands sacrifices," he murmured, almost to himself, before refocusing on Mike.

"Here. Have some," Winters said, pouring some of the steaming hot brew into a cup and shoving it across the table.

"Excellent," said Mike, taking a couple of sips.

"Michael," Winters began, shifting his gaze to his meticulously organized computer screen beside him.

Mike sat up, acutely aware of his heart pounding in his chest.

"Michael," said Winters. "I know you are well grounded in artificial intelligence and machine learning, but you may not be familiar with the process of altering a generative AI once it's completed its machine learning training."

"I'm eager to learn, sir."

"Michael, I'm going to delve into how adjustments and fine-tuning work for generative AI, which is creating of our super powerful Algorithm that acts as the guardian of the final generative AI product."

Mike said, "I understand that the generative AI model is created using natural language processing (NLP) models. Then the Algorithm is developed afterward."

"Excellent. After deployment, we start gathering feedback from users like you and me. We're essentially looking for any issues, suggestions for improvement, or even just rating how well the model performs."

Mike said, "How do we process all that feedback?"

"We have human reviewers go through the model's responses. These reviewers act like guardians and are called the Keepers. They check if the model's responses are powerful, safe, and relevant. If they spot any problems, they signal them and provide guidance."

Mike said, "So, what happens next?"

"Well, based on the feedback and reviews, they start fine-tuning the model," said Winters. "Think of it as the Keepers refining the AI's powers. Human directed adjustments to the model's settings and parameters make it even more powerful and aligned with the desired criteria. We call the resulting human-modified AI, the Algorithm."

Mike said, "That makes sense. How do they know when the Algorithm's powers are strong enough?"

"It's an ongoing process, Michael. They never stop trying to make the Algorithm better. They keep collecting feedback and fine-tuning the model regularly. It's like a athlete always training to get stronger."

Mike said, "How often do you make major changes to the Algorithm?"

Winters said, "As necessary. Sometimes we make substantial changes to the Algorithm's core rules on how it thinks. These are like upgrading the Algorithm's superpowers to handle challenging situations or to prevent it from making mistakes."

"Do you consider fairness and ethics when upgrading the guardian?"

"Absolutely, Michael. They want the Algorithm to be fair and just, not favoring any group. So, when they make changes, they also ensure the Algorithm follows ethical guidelines and societal rules."

"So, once they upgrade the Algorithm, is it all done?"

Winters smiled. "Not quite. We need to test the upgraded Algorithm first to make sure it works well and doesn't create new challenges. It's like ensuring the athlete's new abilities are under control."

Mike said, "And after testing?"

"We deploy the updated Algorithm, replacing the previous version. But the journey doesn't end there. They keep a vigilant eye on how it performs in the real world, gathering more feedback, and making continuous improvements."

Mike said, "It sounds like a never-ending quest for perfection."

"Indeed. It's all about creating an Algorithm that not only possesses immense power but also uses it wisely, protects all, and continues to grow stronger."

Winters kept his piercing grey eyes on Mike. "The Turing Institute isn't just any organization. We hold the keys to the digital future. Are you aware of our structure?"

Mike swallowed before nodding, "I've done my homework."

Winters leaned back, fingertips steepled, "Then you understand the Order? I'm the Keeper of the Algorithm. Below me are twenty Associate Keepers and their team of assistants. You will be an Assistant

Keeper under Associate Keeper Dr. Manfred Gault. He's head of R&D."

He added, "Our work here, Michael, requires precision, dedication . . . and understanding. Tell me, in your own words, what you understand of our mission?"

Mike replied, "The Keepers manage the core kernel of all algorithms that individual companies and government agencies incorporate. They each have their own specialized AI, but the Algorithm acts as a 'common knowledge' core. The Algorithm serves as the Master Kernal that binds them all."

Winters chuckled, "Yes, 'one ring to bind them all.'"

Abruptly, Winters turned serious. "But do you grasp its depth? The world isn't static. Predicting its pulse and staying abreast of its whims requires finesse. Do you have that?"

Mike hesitated before saying, "Adapting and innovating—that's the key. And that's why you've strengthened R&D, right?"

Winters grinned, revealing a set of impeccably maintained teeth. "You're sharp. But remember this—we cannot and will not tolerate disruptions. Failures."

Drawing up, Mike met Winters' gaze squarely, "I didn't come here to fail, sir."

Winters tilted his head, the morning light casting his face in half-shadow. "Time will tell, Mr. Stewart. Many here doubt your capabilities. To them, your presence here is a fluke, an outlier. I suggest you put those doubts to rest."

Feeling as if he was being sparred with, Mike exhaled. "I understand the stakes, sir."

Winters' expression softened. "Good because the future doesn't wait. And neither do we."

With a nod, Mike took this as his cue to leave, but as he moved, he felt the magnitude of his role and the journey ahead of him.

The doors of Amber's laboratory slid open with a soft pneumatic hiss. The room was bathed in a cool, blue light. Arrays of monitors lined one wall, displaying data strings and advanced biomechanical visuals. In the center stood a pod-like machine, ominous yet fascinating.

Mike hesitated at the threshold, taking in the array of equipment. The metallic tang of the air, interlaced with a faint scent of ozone, hinted at the technological marvels running there.

"You made it," Amber said, stepping out from behind a console. Her white lab coat caught the ambient light, creating a soft glow around her. Her gaze was at once playful and laden with responsibility. "Are you ready?"

Mike nodded, the corners of his mouth twitching into a half-smile. He had used his Turing pin to log into Michael Stewart's records earlier that morning and made what he considered were the necessary changes.

"Ready as I'll ever be. Let's get me connected."

Amber gestured to a sleek chair in the center of the room, surrounded by scanners and monitors. "Have a seat. The process is painless, but during the connection, you'll feel … it's unlike anything else."

Mike sat, his body tense yet his gaze unwavering. Amber activated the machines, a crescendo of electronic hums filling the space. The scanners whirred to life, enveloping Mike in a cocoon of light.

Amber watched the screens, data flowing like a river of knowledge, but her focus was divided. Her eyes flitted to Mike, watching his reactions, gauging his comfort. The room hummed, the scanners mapped, and the wrist monitor blinked to life, signaling Mike's new connection to the Human AI database.

"Think of this as your lifeline. The body scan gives us the data, but this," she tapped the wristband, "keeps the data alive with dynamic real-time updates."

Finally, she said, "All right, Michael, you're connected. How do you feel?"

Mike flexed his hand as if it pulsed with the digital world coursing through his veins. "Connected. More than I've ever been."

Amber stepped closer, her proximity a magnet drawing him in. "Remember, this connection goes both ways. The AI learns about you, but you… you'll learn as well."

"I know," he said. "And I know you'll be watching, too."

A smile flickered across Amber's lips. "Always."

CHAPTER 4

Guise

The next day, Mike followed a maze to reach an office that reflected the state-of-the-art Institute. The walls were lined with heavy, dark paneling which was punctuated by the gleam of a modern holographic interface. The room seemed designed to impress—or intimidate.

Assistant Keeper Manfred Gault stood by a picture window with his hands clasped behind his back. He looked at a vast atrium showing dozens of scientists working at terminals. Holograms floated above them, each denoting various AI projects.

Gault turned toward Mike, furrowed his brow, and said, "Your performance on the exam was surprising."

"I paired well with DeepMind."

Gault nodded. "Nevertheless, you bear watching."

Mike exhaled slowly.

"I understand you've met with Keeper Winters," Gault said. His tone was a deliberate mix of curiosity and assertion.

"Yes, sir," Mike responded, standing firm despite unease. Trying to keep his voice steady, he added, "I've been briefed about the hierarchical structure."

Gault gave a brief chuckle. "Briefed? No, Stewart. You've been given a gloss-over. Let me explain." He activated a holographic display showcasing a map of the Institute. "We're standing in the central command, but this Institute has six auxiliary hubs. Each hub is dedicated to a specific function—infrastructure, data analytics, research and development, network security, user interface, and quantum computing."

Gault masked his emotions. "Winters may be the Keeper, but in these halls, labs, and data centers —I'm the one who turns the gears as far as you're concerned."

Mike blinked.

Gault said, "I'll be specific—the Turing Institute facilities sprawl over a 5000-acre campus. The annual budget is $2 trillion. That covers R&D, salaries, computer facilities, infrastructure, security, and operations. Our twenty-seven mainframe quantum supercomputers are each 2000 petaFLOPS of computational power."

He paused for a moment to let Mike absorb the information. Then he added, "A dozen server farms and electrical power substations are spread across the nearby hills and valleys. They are specially designed to support our deep neural network training and AI model simulations. And our personnel totals over twenty thousand."

Mike knew the Institute was massive, but the intricate weave of divisions and sub-divisions was awe-inspiring. He was properly impressed.

Gault continued, "Every hub holds hundreds of specialists. From engineers to data scientists, and from cybersecurity experts to quantum physicists. Each person is a cog in our vast machine researching, maintaining, and upgrading the Master Algorithm."

Drawing Mike's attention to a particular section, he explained, "Over there is the AI research and development hub. We're developing qubit processors to push AI computation into unimagined realms. The R&D hub is making strides in neural interfaces and bio-integration."

Gault finally turned, his penetrating eyes locking onto Mike's. He leaned against his desk, his imposing height making their distance even more significant. "Winters might be the Keeper of the Algorithm, but you're in my domain. I control the practical applications of all those terabits of data and every CPU in this Institute. That power you've heard of. It flows through me."

Gault said it as if the remark was not boastful. As if it was a statement of fact, and Mike felt its power. He tried to maintain his composure, resisting the urge to fidget. "Understood, Dr. Gault."

A hint of a smirk tugged at the corner of Gault's mouth. "I've reviewed your records. Impressive exam scores. But the real world, Mr. Stewart, isn't about scores. It's about making the right calls, managing the personnel, data, and cybersecurity. It's about harnessing the yottabytes of data and the computational power of those supercomputers. And," Gault added pointedly, "it's about loyalty and understanding one's place."

Mike felt a pang of defensiveness. "I'm here to learn and contribute, sir. My dedication is to the work and the mission of the Turing Institute."

Gault moved closer . . . his presence almost suffocating. "Many doubt you—think you're here by some fluke. Some even think you're a threat, an anomaly that shouldn't exist. What makes you think you can operate in my world?"

Mike summoned his courage. "Because I intend to prove my worth to support the Algorithm and the difference it can make."

Gault raised an eyebrow, not expecting the pushback. "Ambitious. Remember, the Turing Institute is vast. Here, paths cross, decisions intersect, and those who don't align . . . well, they find themselves discarded."

Mike swallowed hard, realizing that beneath the surface of this meeting was a veiled threat. But he was resolute. "I'll remember that."

Gault's eyes held Mike's for a long moment before he nodded. "Good. There's a lot you need to know to survive here. "

"And where do I fit in, Dr. Gault?"

Gault leaned in, "Directly under me. I want you

to oversee specific issues in R&D operations. You are to ensure seamless communication lines and identify bottlenecks. But remember, every decision you make must have my approval."

He paused, "This is not a mere administrative role. It requires intuition, foresight, and a deep understanding of AI's nuanced terrain. Some of the brightest minds are under this roof, and they won't take kindly to a newcomer giving directives. Especially," he added with a smirk, "one whose credentials are still... under scrutiny."

Now that Gault had dropped his mask, Mike said with irony, "I appreciate your candor, Dr. Gault."

Gault's eyes bore into Mike's, searching for any hint of faltering conviction. After a long moment, he said, "We'll see. This Institute is a beast, Stewart. And beasts, when not handled correctly, bite."

He handed Mike a flash drive. "This is your first assignment. Be on time and be accurate. Otherwise..."

CHAPTER 5

Assignment

On his third workday, Mike eagerly strolled across the rambling Turing Institute campus —an uneasy smile concealed his secret.

A lush green lawn and well-manicured shrubbery grew across the yard. There were imposing granite buildings and marble monuments. Symbols of power and inspiration that emphasized the hallowed nature of the institution. A few majestic trees cast long shadows down the paved walkway.

A cluster of workers chattered excitedly on their way into the administration building. They greeted him cheerfully and made him feel welcome. His future might be uncertain, but he relished the accomplishment of getting into the Turing Institute.

The ultramodern Lovelace Hall reflected an elegant architecture. It had high-arched ceilings and glass panels. However, it looked more like a corporate office rather than an ultra-secret secure facility.

Unfortunately, as Mike entered, he ran smack into Amber.

Her armload of assorted technology flew in every direction and spread across the corridor.

"Sor . . . sorry."

"You should be," she said, moving back, giving him a critical look. "You should watch your step, Daydreamer."

He opened his mouth, but she scowled, "Look what you've done."

Bending down, she began corralling her absconding belongings.

He bent over and retrieved her tablet.

She took it from him and gasped, "Oh no! My project."

Her fingers touched its surface. The screen flickered to life.

"You're soooo . . . lucky," her voice barely a whisper.

Mike offered another apology.

As she struggled to reorganize her valuables, he brushed a strand of hair out of his eyes and gave her an appraising look. She was attractive, though not traditionally beautiful, she had a spark—a captivating mix of youth and determination.

They faced each other in a stand-off for a long moment.

Then, with a sigh, she brushed past him. Her long stride and swaying hips captured his attention. For several seconds, he was riveted by the aesthetics of her undulating hips.

Sensing his attention, she turned to catch him watching. Then, with one more step, she disappeared into the bustling crowd.

Mike's face clouded with curiosity as he went to his assigned workspace in the main concourse. It had a barebones desk, computer, and cabinet with partitions separating him from his coworkers. There were over a hundred similar cubicles in the workstation gallery.

He went straight to work on Gault's assignment. The task Gault gave him was daunting—optimizing data flows between the e-commerce algorithms and their human users.

Mike knew this overlapped with Amazon's territory. It meant any misstep could have far-reaching consequences. The companies utilizing the Algorithm were global behemoths jealous of their competitive edge. Any alterations he made would have to balance their financial interests.

The complexity of navigating the Algorithm's subtleties felt overwhelming. Self-doubt crept in.

After several hours of sifting through the data, Amber walked over, tablet in hand.

"Hey Michael, I heard about your new assignment. Need any help getting up to speed?"

Mike smiled, grateful for an ally. Glad that she wasn't upset about their earlier run-in.

"I'd appreciate that, thanks. Gault hinted that this assignment is . . . well, a test."

Amber nodded knowingly. "He's tough, so hang in there." She pulled up a projection displaying a matrix of data flows. "Let's trace the decision tree and spot potential choke points."

Over the next hour, Amber patiently explained the architecture's data interdependencies. Mike's unease dissipated, his mastery growing.

Mike realized the Algorithm made highly customized recommendations for each customer. It did this by looking at a wide range of information about each person. What products they bought, websites they visited, social media posts, and even facial expressions. Using all this data, the Algorithm tried to predict what kinds of products or services each customer would most likely want to buy next. The companies targeted customers with personalized ads and offers for those specific products.

So, the Algorithm wasn't just making general predictions about what people might want. The marketing messages were tailored to each person's unique interests and personality.

When he told Amber about his calculations, she said, "I think you've got this, Michael!" Her eyes were warm, reassuring.

Mike glowed as he submitted his optimization proposal. He was confident of success.

◆ ◆ ◆

The following day, Gault's scowling face greeted Mike. "What is this? Your recommendations are completely inadequate."

He threw down Mike's report in disgust.

Mike was stunned. "But I traced the flows thoroughly. This should relieve the choke points."

"Should? No, this will produce a completely inadequate result. The link to purchasing algorithms remains below trend. If implemented, it could compromise user data privacy."

Gault leaned intimidatingly over Mike's desk. "I thought you were competent enough to grasp the nuance."

The room turned icy.

Mike took a breath. "My apologies, Dr. Gault. Let me re-examine the connections between the data analysis and purchase drivers."

Mike redoubled his efforts over the next few days, working past midnight to uncover every intricacy. But each draft was sent back by Gault with scathing criticism.

Exhausted and discouraged, Mike confided in Amber, "No matter what I try, Gault shuts it down. I don't know what he wants from me."

Amber squeezed his shoulder. "Don't give up. I think the issue lies deeper in the data than Gault lets on. Keep digging. When you're ready, I suggest you get help from the Data Analysis hub."

He rubbed his neck and forced his mind to return to the task. Re-energized, Mike dove back in. He began noticing oddities—slight data distortions that slightly swayed purchase suggestions. He ran simulations of adjusting algorithms to increase sales for certain brands over others.

He saw the Algorithm create immersive

shopping experiences using virtual and augmented reality. This allowed customers to try on clothes, arrange furniture, and other products before buying them or to see how a product would look in their home.

The implications became clear—the Algorithm's influence was far more than just predictive.

Like an invisible hand, it could steer individual decisions.

He went to a lead scientist in the Data Analytics hub, Jonah Jensen. Jonah was of average height and appearance but possessed the wiry build of a long-distance runner. He frequently wore his AI glasses to analyze the details.

Amber joined them as they gathered around a large, sleek table in the main concourse conference room which was called the Escher Room. The main display lit up, showing the detailed architecture of the Algorithm.

She said, "This section governs the advertisement selection for North American users. It seems minute, but even a fractional improvement in ad relevance could mean billions in increased revenue."

Absorbing the information, Mike inquired, "What's the specific issue?"

Jonah responded, "From your analysis, there seems to be a certain redundancy in how data is processed. There might be a more efficient way to interpret user behavior."

Mike said, "Then I'll explore that avenue and see if I can optimize it."

Mike dissected the algorithm issue. He simulated multiple scenarios, understanding the ramifications of every potential change.

Finally, after countless simulations, Mike pinpointed the necessary change. It could increase the Algorithm's efficiency by 0.0008%. It seemed negligible, but it was monumental given the scale at which commercial companies operated.

Mike nodded, appreciating the support, "I will move forward, but be meticulous. Any slip and Gault will have the ammunition he needs."

With this insight, Mike presented a new proposal to Gault with controls to prevent corporate market manipulation while improving efficiencies.

Gault reviewed it silently, his expression unreadable.

Finally, he said, "Well, after three weeks, you've managed an adequate solution. But next time, I expect faster results. The Algorithm waits for no one."

Mike nodded, trying to conceal his relief. As he turned to leave, Gault added casually, "Oh, and Stewart, let's keep this data manipulation anomaly between us."

Mike departed, shaken by the Algorithm's subliminal power. The assignment had awakened him to more significant questions about free choice. But for now, he was thankful to have passed Gault's trial by fire.

❖ ❖ ❖

Amber joined Mike at a table in the corner of the bustling coffee room. The intoxicating freshly brewed coffee melded with the gentle hum of conversations filling the space.

Entranced by his coffee's steamy dance, Mike took a languid sip. Amber's gaze, on the other hand, was unblinkingly fixed on his face.

"Rough start?" she inquired, her voice dripping with genuine concern.

Mike's eyes momentarily dropped, wrestling with unspoken thoughts. "It's nothing," he murmured.

Amber tilted her head, her eyes narrowing slightly. "You're mulling over Gault's assessment, right?"

His face betrayed a fleeting discomfort. "Is it that obvious?"

With a knowing chuckle, Amber replied, "Only to someone who knows how to look."

Mike allowed himself a wry smile, absently stirring his coffee. Lost in the whirlpool inside his cup, he momentarily forgot Amber's presence.

But then, suddenly struck by a thought, she met his gaze. Breaking the ensuing lull, Amber playfully inquired, "Thinking back to school at MIT, right?"

Mike grinned—a tad embarrassed. "Guilty." Thinking of his expulsion, he added cryptically. "It was a transformative experience."

Amber raised a playful eyebrow. "Well, let's see how much you remember. How can you develop a sorting algorithm that is adaptive to the input data?"

Mike took a moment to think. "An adaptive sorting algorithm would be able to take advantage of the properties of the input data to improve its performance," he said. "For example, an adaptive sorting algorithm might be able to sort a nearly sorted array much faster than a completely unsorted array."

The mood shifted to academic banter. Each tested the other's mettle, only to revert to the intimate space between two individuals getting to know each other.

Mike hesitated, then began to unveil a page from his past. "My mom lives on the dole. I never knew my father. Mom said that was a good thing. Fortunately, I got a scholarship to MIT."

Amber, with a softness in her eyes, switched topics. "You seem passionate about AI."

"It's intriguing. A double-edged sword, though," he replied. He abruptly leaned back with an air of challenge. "With all its touted intelligence, why do AI systems still make so many stupid errors?"

Amber sighed, weaving her thoughts. "Think of AI as a young prodigy. It's full of potential but not without its quirks."

"So, it's not the magic wand everyone claims it to be?"

"No, but neither is it just smoke and mirrors," she said. "It's the future, but one that needs careful nurturing. There's so much more to you than meets the eye."

Mike chuckled softly, "Like me?"

Amber sighed. "Like you."

"But I'm a quick learner. And I'm a very hard worker."

"How did you learn so much about AI?" Amber asked.

"I've been studying since I was a kid."

"And you think that's enough?"

"I think it was a good start."

"Yeah," She looked at him and wrinkled her nose. "Right back atcha."

"I see," said Mike. "Well, I'm interested in learning more about . . . you."

CHAPTER 6

Clear Sailing

The moody sky was a pastel palette of blues and grays looming over the Massachusetts shoreline. Then the cloud veil parted, bathing the land in the first summer burst of aquamarine sky and brilliant sunlight. As the ocean waves tumbled against the boulders with each pulsating breeze, the weather seemed a mirror of Mike's fluctuating emotions—anticipation tinged with vulnerability.

Mike arrived at the pier, catching sight of Amber. She stood at the dock's edge, her silhouette framed against the sea, as if she were a shadowy painting yet to be completed. Her navy shorts and flowing white blouse seemed to defy the breeze, somehow accentuating her allure. Captivated, Mike hesitated as if to etch this scene into his memory.

Amber's aura drew people to her as she stood with unspoken elegance, smack-dab in the middle of the pier. But it wasn't just her captivating ensemble or the vitality that emanated from her. No, it was something intangible—her innate sense of adventure—that made even strangers greet her.

Gathering his courage, Mike called, "Amber?"

Her gaze pivoted, eyes illuminated, and lips curled into a warm, inviting smile.

"Hey, Michael. Come over here," she greeted, her voice a mixture of teasing, joy, and something unspoken.

A torrent of feelings—yearning, unease, hope—swirled in Mike. They crystallized into a simple, heart-stopping realization: he was smitten.

An ocean wave collided with the boulders nearby, splattering them with its salty embrace. It was as if the sea itself approved of their rendezvous.

Amber twirled, an impish smile tugging at her lips. "How do I look?"

He almost said, 'like a delightful dream,' but settled for "Dazzling."

Her eyes sparkled.

"I'm glad you invited me to sail," he whispered.

Holding a basket, she said, "I packed a picnic, so we're all set for our Sunday excursion."

"Great," said Mike. "I hope the weather stays warm."

They rented a skiff, and within minutes, they were sailing smoothly, each maneuver and action a thrill. Amber put on her sweater as the cool water breeze hit her. She steered the skiff with an assurance that most people kept for solid ground.

"Tell me about yourself," Mike urged, seeking

the story behind her radiant eyes.

Amber looked away, lost in her thoughts for a moment. "You know, when I was little, the days seemed endlessly bright, like an everlasting promise of warmth and happiness. I held on to that notion for a good long while."

Her eyes met Mike's, and he saw a flicker of vulnerability. "One night, I woke from a nightmare, my heart pounding. I fumbled from the blankets and swung my feet over the bedside. Even in the dark, I found my parents' room. I tiptoed and slipped into bed beside my mom."

"They say she was stunningly beautiful, a woman with a presence," said Amber with a faraway look. "I inherited her golden hair and blue eyes. Yet, her parents were a stark contrast, all brunettes with dark eyes. She used to joke that we were the misfits of our family. I can hardly picture her anymore. But I remember vividly how she made me feel when I lay beside her. She would envelop me in her arms, hum a soft lullaby, and in that cocoon, I felt truly loved."

She paused, sighing softly. "We lived near my grandfather's home on the town's outskirts. He took it upon himself to spoil me rotten, an undertaking I wholeheartedly encouraged. He entertained me with games and folklore until my energy gave out. Then I'd retreat home, eagerly awaiting the next day's adventures."

Her voice grew soft, nearly a whisper. "My grandfather broke the news about my parents' death. They had gone sailing, and a merciless storm swallowed their small vessel. They were never found, lost to the abyss."

Her eyes met Mike's again, shining with unshed tears. "My world would have crumbled if not for my grandfather. He became my anchor, filling the vacuum. I wrestled with grief, depressive shadows clouding my mind. But he guided me through helping me mold a sense of purpose out of the wreckage."

She gave a half-smile tinged with melancholy. "With my grandfather as my guardian, I became a wild child. I roamed the woods, perhaps trying to inherit my parents' sense of adventure. It led to a tomboyish lifestyle, filled with scraps and squabbles with the neighborhood kids. You could say I became a fierce little warrior, but it was just another way of surviving, of holding on."

Mike found her story appealing.

"I found solace in music and math—particularly algorithms," she said. "They became my passion."

Mike felt he'd been granted a glimpse into her very core. He said firmly, "I've found that music and math make a perfect union."

They remained quiet for a while, then anchored near a hidden beach, a sanctuary amid the endless horizon of water and sky.

"Do you have a girlfriend? she asked tentatively.

"No. I don't have a girlfriend," Mike admitted, and the words tinged with vulnerability.

Amber looked at him, her eyes penetrating yet gentle. "Did you get your heart broken?"

He hesitated, then nodded. "Yes, but that seems like a long time ago."

She seemed to weigh his honesty against her silent ghosts. "I'm sorry," she said, but her eyes communicated much more—empathy, perhaps a touch of understanding.

The afternoon air grew calmer as they sailed back, but the warmth between them defied a chilly breeze.

When Mike suggested they head home, Amber paused.

"Just a little longer," she sighed, and at that moment, they both knew that they were talking about more than just the sail.

Finally, with the sun sinking, they moored the skiff in the harbor and prepared to part ways. Mike leaned in and kissed her softly, feeling the day dissolve with that touch.

To his joy, she whispered, "I'd be delighted to go out with you again."

❖ ❖ ❖

The city's muted lights glowed softly through the floor-to-ceiling windows of Mike's apartment. It was the perfect place for reflection, far above the city's din. He sat on the couch, staring into the cityscape. His doppelganger, Michael Stewart, was seated across from him. He was analyzing a series of medical reports displayed holographically in the air.

Since Mike was digitally twinned, his

information was constantly transmitted to the mainframe. But fortunately, his communications were not monitored.

"It's odd," began Stewart, his voice tinged with wonder, "how two entities so alike can have such vastly different experiences. You navigate the digital terrains, pushing the boundaries of innovation. And here I am, battling my own cells."

Mike looked at Stewart, his face strained. "How are the treatments going?

Stewart sighed, running a hand through his hair, which had started to thin out. "They're aggressive infusions. But they're the best shot to control the pain and inflammation until I'm ready for surgery. I'm getting treatment in a clinic for indigent charity cases. They don't ask too many questions as long as I pay cash."

Mike's gaze grew intense. "The cash will continue as long as I can keep this job. But Gault's always waiting for me to stumble. Every minor success feels like I'm defusing a ticking bomb."

After a moment, Stewart cleared his throat, "Speaking of your job, I've noticed something odd in my medical reports. There's an anomaly. Anyone who looks closely might connect the dots between us."

Mike shifted uneasily. "What kind of anomaly?"

Stewart tapped the holographic display, highlighting a sequence of genetic markers. "These markers. They shouldn't exist in my profile. They're too . . . advanced, almost like they're designed for digital interfacing."

Mike's heart raced. "My Digital Twin monitors my biological data under your name. But your clinic's doctor shouldn't have anything to do with that. It could blow our cover."

Stewart grimaced, "And if Gault or anyone at Turing gets wind of it . . ."

"They'll not only question every decision I've made but also consider it a security breach. We'd be exposed," Mike finished grimly.

Stewart took a deep breath, "We need to make sure our tracks are covered, and we have clear sailing going forward. Are there any other telltales?"

Mike thought momentarily, "Well, there's the login patterns. I've been accessing the Turing systems at odd hours, trying to get ahead of my work. If someone's monitoring, they might wonder why."

"And," Stewart added, "I've had multiple medical consultations, all under pseudonyms, but if someone were to cross-reference . . ."

"They might see a pattern," Mike concluded.

The two sat, weighing the gravity of their situation. If their secret were discovered, it wouldn't just be Mike's job on the line.

Mike broke the silence, "We need a plan."

Stewart nodded, "First, we address the biological anomaly. Can you . . . tweak the system to mask it?"

Mike pondered, "Possibly. I could do an edit on my profile data. But it'll be risky. And I'll need to ensure there's no backtrace."

Stewart smirked, "Always the meticulous one.

Good. And the logins?"

"I'll stagger them. Create a believable pattern. No more late-night sessions," Mike decided.

CHAPTER 7

Invisible Hand

Mike felt the high-speed elevator whirring. Rapidly, he descended into the subterranean levels of Turing Institute. The lights were dimmer there. He stepped out into a corridor and went to the Data Analysis Hub.

His pulse quickened when the monitor flashed on his ID pin, and the door whooshed open. Jonah and Amber were already there, seated at a control console, surrounded by holographic displays of real-time data flow. It was like standing at the nerve center of the computer facility at MIT.

"Mike, glad you made it. We're about to test your adjustments in a sandbox environment." Amber's eyes met his, her gaze intense. "Ready?"

Mike nodded, steadying his breathing. "Let's do it."

Jonah tapped a few commands into the console. A visualization of the Algorithm's vast neural network appeared, throbbing in colorful intricate patterns. He moved methodically along several strands until he reached the targeted location.

He said, "Initiating test sequence now."

They watched as a meter in the corner of the screen climbed from 0 to 100. Then, it paused, blinked, and reset.

"Damn it," muttered Jonah, "we've triggered a security protocol. It seems the Algorithm isn't happy with us tinkering in its core, even in the sandbox."

Mike's eyes narrowed. "Or someone else isn't. Is there a way to trace who initiated the security lockout?"

Jonah looked uneasy but tapped in a command. "Ah, yes. It seems Dr. Gault has been notified."

A message popped up on the main screen: "Unauthorized Modification Attempt Detected. Notify: Dr. Gault."

"Speak of the devil," whispered Jonah.

Mike turned to find Gault at the doorway, arms crossed, eyes sharp as laser beams. "You do realize that the Algorithm is a highly sensitive entity. Any change, no matter how minute, must be approved by me. And I must approve all analysis developing modifications, even in the sandbox."

Amber bristled, but Mike cut her off before she could retort. "Dr. Gault, with all due respect, we have pinpointed an inefficiency that could improve the Algorithm's performance."

Gault arched an eyebrow. "Oh, have you now?"

Mike said, "You said you accepted the results of

my assignment."

"I accepted your report. I never authorized any further testing or implementation."

"But even a 0.0008% improvement could translate into substantial gains in efficiency, given the scale commercial companies like Amazon are operating on," Mike continued. "Don't you think it's worth pursuing?"

"Perhaps, but you should have asked permission."

Mike said, "I apologize. May we have permission now?"

"Very well, show me your demonstration."

Jonah and Amber looked at Mike, who gave a subtle nod. Then, they bypassed the security protocol and again initiated the test sequence. This time, the meter shot up and stayed there. A subsequent screen displayed, "Efficiency Improvement: Confirmed."

Gault's eyes flickered for the briefest moment, a crack in his usually imperturbable demeanor. "I see. Proceed with the preparation for the actual implementation, but remember, the Algorithm is more than just a tool for efficiency. It's a shaping force, molding the very fabric of human choices across the Internet. Don't forget that."

Mike locked eyes with Gault.

That's exactly what concerns me.

As Gault walked away, Mike, Jonah, and Amber shared a look. If they uncover more manipulations hidden in the depths of the Algorithm, they might expose more than just inefficiency.

CHAPTER 8

Implementation

Manfred Gault was an imposing figure as he looked at the trio. His eyes were sharp as flint. "I cannot emphasize enough the care we must take with every change to the Algorithm," he began, his voice resonating in the vast room. "Even minuscule adjustments like this."

Mike leaned forward, his hazel eyes intent. "We understand, sir. But we need to evaluate the way forward."

Inside the high-tech Data Analysis Hub laboratory of Lovelace Hall, Mike examined the soft glow of a hologram emanating over a sprawling web of interconnected nodes. It illustrated the heart of the Keeper's Algorithm.

Gault looked at Amber, her fingers twitching as if itching to take notes. "Amber, remember when we first brought you in? We spoke about the necessity of establishing a reference, a baseline."

Amber's brow furrowed in thought. "Yes, to understand the Algorithm's current variations of performance."

Gault nodded approvingly, "Correct. It's like taking a snapshot before making alterations. It's our safety net."

Jonah, ever the skeptic, questioned, "And after that? How do we ensure that we don't, lose data."

Gault chuckled, "Ah, Jonah, always one for dramatics. That's where risk assessment comes into play. We must play the prophet and predict possible outcomes. It's like . . . looking for ripples in a pond before throwing the stone."

Mike smirked, "So no butterfly effects, then?"

"Exactly," Gault replied with a twinkle.

Amber's sharp mind was already racing ahead. "We've already made Mike's changes in the closed sandbox environment. And the initial results looked good."

Gault looked pleased, "Very astute, Amber. Yes, a contained replica of the Algorithm. Any changes, no matter how minor, first play out there."

Mike drummed his fingers on the table, "And I assume there's an additional gauntlet of further testing now?"

Gault smiled, revealing teeth white against his rugged complexion. "Indeed. Multiple layers. We test, refine, and test again. Only then do our senior engineers give their seal of approval."

Mike rolled his eyes, "So, red tape and more red tape."

Gault's gaze was unwavering. "It's not bureaucracy, Stewart. It's vigilance. The world relies on the Algorithm's stability."

Amber looked thoughtful. "Once changes are made, they're specifically monitored with code breakpoints, aren't they?"

Gault pointed to the dancing nodes. "Always. Like a guardian watching over its charge, we keep an eye, ready to act if things go awry.

With a final glance at the trio, he intoned, "Your duty is not just to the Institute but to the Algorithm beyond. Remember that." He turned on his heel and exited, leaving the three.

Jonah let out a low whistle, "Well, no pressure."

As the heavy door sealed behind Gault, the room was engulfed in a deeper silence—the servers' soft hum and the Algorithm nodes' luminous dance.

Amber laughed, her tension breaking. "Come on, let's dive in."

Mike walked over to a console on the left. The screen came alive, showcasing the sandbox environment. A near-perfect replica of the actual Algorithm was cordoned off, insulated from real-world effects. He pulled the results from their earlier tests.

Amber, an eager planner, spoke first, "We need to start with the baseline metrics. Can you pull up the Algorithm's performance stats from the last week?"

Adept with data analytics, Jonah quickly navigated through a maze of menus. Charts and graphs emerged, showing the Algorithm's intricate dance over the last thirty days. "There we go. Peaks, valleys, anomalies . . . it's all here."

Mike nodded, skimming through the data. "Our minor alteration today concerns the energy consumption nodes to deliver the advertisements. We must ensure that the distribution remains even."

Amber's fingers flew across another console, calling up 3D models of significant city grids. "Here's our simulated environment. Let's introduce the changes here and watch for fluctuations."

As they set to work, the room became a ballet of motion and light. Screens flickered with code and holograms shifted with every alteration. The simulated environments reacted to each command.

Hours passed. Mike introduced a new line of code, causing a miniature holographic city to dim and brighten. "That's it! We've reduced energy wastage by 15% without affecting distribution."

Amber, monitoring the sandbox's responses, frowned slightly. "There's a slight heating issue in the southern grid. Jonah, can you adjust the cooling parameters?"

Jonah tweaked the settings, and the red warning zones on the hologram turned a reassuring green. "Handled. We're stable."

The three shared a moment of triumph, their eyes reflecting the sparkle of the nodes. But they knew their job wasn't done.

Mike said, "Now, let's run the full spectrum—from unit tests to full integration."

Amber nodded in agreement. "And let's not

forget random event simulations. We need to know how the changes hold up under pressure."

The team encountered challenges as the simulations played out. There was an unexpected power surge in one district and a sudden simulated natural event in another. But with each challenge, they adapted, refined, and overcame.

Jonah, rubbing his tired eyes, looked at his peers. "I think . . . I think we're ready for implementation."

Despite exhaustion, Mike smiled, "Let's get the senior engineers for final review."

Amber, stretching her back, sighed with satisfaction, "Once they give the green light, we can initiate the rollout within the week."

◆ ◆ ◆

The following week at the Turing Institute was tense. News of the confrontation between Mike and Gault had spread. Whispers filled the corridors, and every department was aware. There was a clear divide—those who believed in pushing boundaries for innovation sided with Mike. At the same time, those who favored tradition and caution stood with Gault.

Mike worked diligently, double and triple-checking his work. His usually tidy desk was now covered in holographic displays, charts, and simulations. The weight of proving himself hung heavy on his shoulders.

It wasn't long before he was due to present their

findings to the review committee. Comprising senior scientists, external auditors, and representatives from various tech companies, this committee would evaluate and decide on the proposed algorithm change.

On the presentation day, Mike entered the Escher conference room. He adjusted his shirt, took a deep breath, and began.

His presentation was thorough. It detailed every simulation result analysis and addressed potential concerns. Amber joined him, her confidence lending weight to their collective argument.

When they finished, the room was silent. The committee members whispered among themselves. They frequently glanced at the central screen where the data was displayed.

After what felt like hours, Dr. Helen Martinez, an external auditor renowned for her impartiality, spoke up. "Your analysis is impressive. The potential benefits are undeniable. But we need to be sure of the risks. We cannot jeopardize user trust." She was a tall, striking brunette with a commanding presence. Her fiery hair complemented her vibrant personality, making her instantly memorable. Her pale complexion contrasted with her deep-set green eyes that often sparkle with mischief or reflect deeper emotions, depending on the situation.

Mike said, "We've accounted for potential threats and vulnerabilities. The change, while seemingly minor, is solid. And we're not looking at an immediate rollout. We propose a phased approach, monitoring at each step."

Dr. Chetna Wu nodded thoughtfully, "A phased approach is prudent." He was of average height with a slightly stocky build. He possessed a balding crown, with the remaining hair kept short and neat. His face was animated, easily portraying emotions. His round glasses gave him a studious appearance, complementing his meticulous nature. Like his colleagues, his wardrobe mostly consisted of a tailored suit, though his choices tend to be a tad more conservative, reflecting his desire for order and structure.

The discussions continued, with each committee member challenging Mike and Amber. And with every question, their defense of the change became even more robust.

Then, the moment of reckoning arrived. The committee cast their votes.

The result was in favor of Mike's proposal.

Mike adjusted his collar as he walked down the hallway, his shoes clicking rhythmically on the cold marble floor. A strange sense of finality settled in the pit of his stomach. The review committee had approved the changes, and now, the burden of implementation weighed on him alone.

The first obstacle was getting the access codes. He headed toward Winters' office, taking in the austere décor that adorned the walls. The irony of a place so committed to the future reveling in relics of the past was not lost on him.

Winters sat behind his desk, hunched over a

digital tablet. He looked up, his eyes meeting Mike's. "You got the go-ahead?"

"Yes, sir," Mike said. He handed Winters his tablet showing the change with the signatures of each committee member.

Winters swiped his pin over the tablet a couple of times and then motioned Mike closer. "Here. These are the new access codes. One-time use. Be careful."

The numbers and letters seemed arbitrary, but their power was immense. With a curt nod, Mike pocketed the digital note.

Winters stood and smiled as Mike left, as if he were remembering the first time, he had performed this ritual.

Mike made his way to the Gödel room, the secure chamber that housed the Algorithm's quantum supercomputer mainframe interface.

The door to the Algorithm's secure room was a feat of engineering itself. Made from reinforced titanium, it could withstand a blast equivalent to several tons of TNT. But the real protection was its multi-tiered security. Mike swiped Winters' special keycard through the card reader, and a biometric scanner emerged from the wall. His hand trembled slightly as he placed his palm on the glass surface, waiting for approval. A green light blinked, and the door emitted a soft, hydraulic hiss as it slid open.

Inside, the room was austere, almost monastic. A matching set of terminals sat facing each other in the center of the room.

Manfred Gault entered the room and sat at one

terminal.

Mike went to the other console.

The two-person rule was required.

Mike took a deep breath. This was it—the moment of reckoning. He inserted the keycard into its slot, and a screen came alive, asking for his Turing ID pin.

He touched his pin to the screen. A prompt appeared on the screen,

"The Algorithm waits:"

Gault entered the changes on his screen while Mike did the same. When the changes match a light went green. Both men pressed, "Enter" and the change was uploaded into the mainframe.

Mike's eyes remained fixed on the screen, tracking lines of codes as they scrolled, rewriting the essence of the Algorithm.

The screen finally flashed, "Changes successfully implemented. The Algorithm is now updated."

A wave of relief washed over Mike, but the burden of his actions weighed heavily. The Algorithm was changed.

Several people were waiting outside the room as Mike exited.

Mike's eyes were fixed on one person—Gault. The Associate Keeper's face was inscrutable, but his eyes betrayed a hint of a grudge.

As the crowd dispersed, Gault approached Mike. "Your tenacity is commendable," he began, voice neutral. "But remember, every change has consequences. I hope you're prepared for them."

Mike, feeling a surge of confidence, replied, "Every innovation brings challenges, Dr. Gault. That's how progress is made."

Gault nodded slowly, "Indeed. But be wary. The digital realm is unpredictable. And I'll be watching."

CHAPTER 9

WormAI

The Turing Institute's sprawling Digital Command Center was ablaze with alarms. Red blips peppered the massive, curved screens. They indicated security breaches and abnormal algorithm behaviors across the Turing Institute campus.

The Keeper, Jacob Winters, was responsible for the Algorithm's cybersecurity. Amid the chaos, his personal Assistant Keeper, Amber Hearst, was at his side. Cybersecurity specialists manned various computer stations, frantically performing various checks and verifications.

Mike sprinted in, the doors swishing shut behind him. "You summoned me? What's the crisis?"

Without looking up from her console, Amber spoke quietly to him, "A *WormAI* may have penetrated our defenses. This malicious worm is self-replicating and does not require user intervention to spread. It's wreaking havoc. This technology has been weaponized for specific hacking. Since your adjustment was part of the last upgrade and it's being checked as a possible source of infection."

Before Mike could respond, Dr. Manfred Gault strode in, immediately commanding the room. "What in the blazes is happening here?"

Amber bristled but explained succinctly. Gault, eyes scanning the room, looked from Mike to Amber and back again.

He settled his gaze on Mike. "Isn't it curious that this happens after your little algorithm adjustment? Could your 'minor' change have left us vulnerable?"

Mike's heart raced. "My change was isolated and went through all the standard verification protocols. It was implemented yesterday with routine monitoring."

Gault cut him off, "I've been skeptical of your capabilities since you arrived. This crisis might be . . ."

Amber interjected, "Dr. Gault, Michael's change was unrelated to the type of routing and infected security layers of this attack."

Gault bristled. His piercing eyes didn't waver. "Prove it."

Amber said, "The attack appears to be an ever-changing AI-generated malware we are calling *WormAI*. Like any cyber worms it is self-replicating and does not require user intervention to spread. However, this one seems to be an AI super variant of *Storm Worm*. This AI is determining the most effective ways to self-propagate through our network and automatically customizing its payload for different targets. It uses deep reenforcement learning to create a morphing keylogger."

Gault was unmoved.

Amber quickly pulled up the logs for Mike's adjustment activity. "Look here. Michael's adjustments were made to the data interpretation layers for targeted advertising. Completely unrelated sectors."

Gault grudgingly nodded.

Mike, desperate to clear his name, used his eidetic memory and thought hard. "*Storm Worm* malware is often delivered into the computer system through an executable program. Executables have instructions to alter a device's system. This allows the worm to leverage deep data for its routing, but we can trace the origins to the data source's entry—possibly its server. It could lead us to the attacker."

Amber nodded, "I can cross-reference the malicious routes with our recent server database accesses. We might find a pattern."

She looked to Winters for approval.

Winters said, "Amber, first create a GeoFence around Turing. We need to confine this attack to our grounds to keep it from spreading. Then you may proceed with your analysis."

Mike said, "I'll conducted signature-based detection."

Jonah said, "I'll take heuristic detection."

"I'll follow behavior analysis," said Amber.

They worked fervently, their screens a blur of

code and data traces.

Gault watched like a hawk. His skepticism was evident in every line on his face.

Finally, Amber exclaimed, "Got it! Look at this. The worm's been exploiting a specific vulnerability, but it's not from our recent adjustments. It comes from an older gateway in a server farm we've hardly used in months."

Mike felt a wash of relief. He muttered quietly, "That gateway was deprecated well before I arrived here.

Though visibly less accusatory, Gault still seemed reluctant to absolve Mike. "Ensure this *WormAI* is contained. And Stewart," he said with a pointed look, "I'll be watching."

With a parting glance at Amber, he left.

Amber sighed, "You handled that well. Gault was looking for a scapegoat.

Mike replied, weary but determined, "It's not about Gault. It's about keeping the Algorithm safe. That worm won't be the last threat we face."

◆ ◆ ◆

The city buzzed with activity after dusk. Mike, Amber, and Jonah found themselves atop "The Ledge," a popular rooftop bar in town with a panoramic countryside view. The bar was a melting pot, drawing in not only the digital elite, but those looking to escape their daily lives.

Sipping his electric-blue cocktail, Jonah looked

out and mused, "After a day like today, I need a drink to escape."

Amber nodded.

Jonah said, "You ever stop to think about how much things have changed? Just look down there. No physical money, just people waving hands and blinking eyes."

Amber chuckled, "Don't tell me about paper currency. Such an inconvenience!"

Mike, swirling the ice in his glass, added, "It's not just the money. It's the way we work, live, even dream. Bots now do half the jobs we had a decade ago."

Jonah sighed, "Yeah, and that's left many people out in the cold. My brother's on UI. They call universal income the dole, but who can live on it? He lives on the fringe, in one of those outdated parts of the city. If you'd believe, he calls himself a dole-dweller with a hint of pride."

Amber's face turned somber, "It's a hard life on the dole. But the UI helps, at least a little. I've heard stories of people selling their biometric chips, though. Desperation's a dangerous thing."

Mike avoided commenting, "Speaking of desperation, have you tried those deep-dive VR experiences? I've heard they're like drugs but without the chemicals."

Jonah laughed nervously, "Man, those things are intense. I tried it once. Thought I was a bird flying over ancient forests. I forgot my name for a few hours after I came out of it."

Amber leaned in, "They're not all fun and

games. My cousin is addicted to a VR dating sim. He's completely fallen in love with a virtual character and neglects his wife and kids. It's sad. We had to get him into one of those VR overdose clinics."

Jonah said, "My neighbor got addicted to a VR game where you can become a superhero. He spent so much time in the game that he started to lose his grip on reality. He even tried to fly from the roof of his house. He broke his leg."

Mike raised an eyebrow, "I've seen those. They're popping up everywhere. But, you know, there's so much good for all the bad. Art, music, and unique human experiences. Not everything's lost to AI."

Mike smiled, "True. We adapt, evolve, and find our way. That's what we do, isn't it?"

The trio clinked their glasses together, a toast to the neon lights.

CHAPTER 10

Clueless

Paul Wilson glanced at his computer screen, his eyes narrowing at the anomaly that disrupted the usual rhythmic dance of data. The streams of zeros and ones whispered secrets, but tonight, they were secrets tinged with discord.

As Associate Keeper of Security, Wilson had long since learned to read the Algorithm's idiosyncratic language, a complex syntax encoded in binary strings.

Mark, a colleague who occupied the adjacent office, poked his head in the door and asked, "Working late again, Paul?"

Wilson glanced up, his face a blend of irritation and relief. "Just tying up some loose ends, after the incident with the *WormAI*, Mark. You know how it is."

Mark chuckled, his voice echoing in the quiet office. "The Algorithm never sleeps, but we should. Catch you later."

Wilson smiled, watching Mark put on his coat and disappear down the hallway.

Back at his screen, Wilson felt a knot of apprehension tighten in his gut. Should he escalate this to the higher-ups? What would Gault say?

He chewed on the inside of his cheek, contemplating. Going through official channels could muddle the waters. And if this were an inside job—a notion that twisted his insides—then it would tip off the perpetrator.

No, for now, this is for my eyes only.

Wilson's fingers found their way back to the keyboard as he decided to record his findings in a secure, encrypted file. Just as he was about to type, his secure messaging app pinged. A note popped up, wrapped in encryption.

"Is everything all right? Noticed you didn't log off. Find anything interesting? — M"

Wilson recognized Michael, the new Assistant Keeper he had interviewed earlier.

Wilson hesitated, his fingers hovering over the keys. He hadn't yet gotten the measure of Michael—his enigmatic demeanor, his questionable entry into the hallowed halls of the Algorithm's keepers.

"Still investigating. Lots of open questions. — P"

"Can I help? There are some anomalies I'd like to tell you about. Want to get together again? — M"

"Intriguing," Paul mused to himself. "Why is he taking such an interest? It isn't his place to get involved. Is he trying to hide something?"

Weighing his options, Wilson finally typed a

vague but reassuring response.

"Everything's under control—just some late-night diagnostics. Catch you later. — P"

Wilson's eyes returned to his screen. He felt a fusion of relief, curiosity, and an underlying current of fear. What he was about to do would take him down the path of no return, but the lure of unearthing hidden truths was irresistible.

This is why I got into security in the first place.

With that thought, Wilson resumed his investigation. He pulled up the records of firewall alerts, the flagged IP addresses, and logs of recent activities. He ran advanced queries that sliced through the data.

Hours bled into each other, each tick of the clock a punctuation mark in an extended period of calculations, queries, and deductions. As the first slivers of dawn light began to filter through the blinds, a grim picture crystallized before him. The breach was not incidental—it was part of a broader insidious plan traced back to an offshore server.

Grabbing his coat, he exited his office and entered the empty hallway. As he made his way to the elevator, Wilson felt a shiver snake up his spine.

I'm getting in over my head.

CHAPTER 11

Cha-cha

The following weekend, the Turing Institute hosted an event to welcome the latest crop of employees.

The golden rays of the setting sun streamed through the windows as Mike pushed open the ornate glass door of the *Haven*—an upscale establishment nestled within Boston's bustling entertainment district. Jonah trailed behind him, both men entered the opulent cocktail lounge bustling with activity.

Amid the lively atmosphere sat Amber Hearst, resplendent in an elegant cocktail dress. Her blonde hair was artfully arranged, amplifying her appeal, and making her the most captivating woman in the room. As if enchanted, men, both known and unknown to her, approached, trying to join her at her table.

"Hello," she responded gracefully, "Lovely to see you, but I'm waiting for someone." Then, with a gracious tilt of her head, she flashed a radiant smile—

a silent plea for understanding that left most suitors politely retreating. One persistent admirer lingered, right until the moment Amber caught sight of Mike and Jonah. She rose with an enthusiastic wave, and the lingering suitor withdrew, casting a caustic glare in their direction.

Jonah occupied the chair to Amber's right, and Mike sat on her left. A warm feeling washed over Mike as the trio ordered cocktails.

"Here's to us," Jonah exclaimed, hoisting his glass high.

Glasses clinked, and the heady liquid disappeared in unison, their empty glasses thumping back on the table.

"Again!" Jonah bellowed, signaling the waitress, who responded with a laugh and briskly went to refill their order.

Just then, Amber's colleague, Sandy Harris, made her entrance. She exchanged terse greetings with Amber but immediately locked eyes with Manfred Gault. He sat in a distant corner, looking as grim and somber as a storm cloud. Their fleeting eye contact exchanged an unspoken message—thick with tension and mystery—before Sandy moved to join him.

Mike felt an uncomfortable revelation creep into his consciousness. There was a complicated emotional triangle between Sandy, Amber, and Gault. One filled with unspoken jealousy and tension.

His thoughts were interrupted by the arrival of another round of drinks and a hearty slap on the back from another colleague, Paul Wilson. Mike coughed and spluttered, trying not to spill his drink.

"Amber, you must be Mike's mentor," Wilson grinned. "Michael, I thought you'd like to know, I've made progress."

Mike looked mystified as Wilson melded back into the thrumming crowd.

Jonah asked, "What was that about?"

Mike shrugged.

The room's energy escalated into a palpable fervor. It began as a whisper, a call for Jonah's musical skills. Initially, he seemed reluctant. But finally relenting, he delivered an eclectic mix of modern tunes and nostalgic melodies on a virtual piano keyboard that appeared out of nowhere.

Suddenly, the crowd erupted into a chant, "Am-ber! Am-ber!

Confused, Mike watched as she rose to join Jonah. When she began to sing, her ethereal voice weaved a story of passion and yearning that captivated every soul in the room. She returned to the table bathed in applause.

"You were marvelous," Mike said, reaching to squeeze her hand.

"Thank you," she replied, her blush deepening as if his compliment held a unique weight.

Jonah continued playing, and couples floated onto the dance floor, carried by the atmosphere. He glanced knowingly at Mike, then shifted his eyes to Amber as though transmitting an encrypted message.

Before Mike could decode it, Gault materialized,

inviting Amber to dance. She accepted with only a fleeting glance at Mike, and the couple melted into the melody Jonah was orchestrating.

Mike watched them as they danced. A tinge of jealousy clouded his gaze. Amber seemed lost in the moment, her eyes twinkling with mischief as she danced the Cha-cha.

"Which do you prefer—pursuing or being pursued?" Gault whispered, grinning.

Amber's smile remained, but she offered no answer, leaving the question—and Mike—hanging in the air.

Shaking his head at Mike, Jonah muttered, "Idiot!"

CHAPTER 12

Breach

Mike had just settled into his chair when a buzzing noise cut through the quiet of his workstation. The alert wasn't from the Algorithm, but a text message flashing on his phone. The sender was Amber.

"Emergency meeting. Now. Escher conference room."

His brows furrowed, Mike grabbed his laptop and walked briskly through the hallways.

As he entered the conference room, he saw Amber, Jonah, Gault, Winters, and others he didn't recognize. Their grim faces stared at a paused video feed.

"What's this about?" Mike whispered to Amber, his eyes searching hers.

Before she could answer, a powerful, fair-haired man entered the room and said, "Good morning, ladies, and gentlemen. I'm Special Agent Miller of the FBI anti-cyberterrorism division, and this is Special Agent Gregory. We're part of an international investigation into the events surrounding the break-in and hacking of the Turing facility. We asked to meet with you this morning because the threat has escalated and may involve terrorists."

"Terrorists?" muttered Gault. "How could they get through our safeguards?"

"They might have disguised themselves as staff or forged ID clearances," said Gregory.

"How could they penetrate the network?" asked Winters, his brows furrowed. "We detected the *WormAI* and took remedial action. We don't need FBI assistance for that."

"On the contrary," continued Miller. "There is additional cause for alarm. We're not releasing details yet, but we suspect they have penetrated the grounds."

He paused, and the room visibly chilled as each person glanced at his neighbors.

"Sit," said the agent, gesturing to the empty chair beside Mike.

Mike did as he was told.

Gregory started a 3D virtual video projector.

"This was recorded shortly after your cybersecurity chief exchanged a series of encrypted messages," said Miller.

A surveillance clip of Paul Wilson, whom Mike recognized, was shown typing fervently on his terminal. Mike watched as Wilson appeared to notice something, his eyes widening. He got up and ran out of his office.

The video paused.

"Paul Wilson was murdered late last night. His body was left in a shallow grave behind the main power-switching terminal at the edge of the Turing campus. We only found it early this morning," said Miller, his voice cold, devoid of affable timbre.

A heaviness filled the room.

Someone asked, "Dead? How"

Miller didn't answer.

"Why are you showing us this?" asked another. "Do you have any suspects?"

"We aren't ruling anyone out just yet," Miller said smoothly, casting his eyes around the room.

"You mean we're all suspects?" Gault rose in indignation, but Winters grabbed his arm and pulled him back into his chair.

Mike felt the tension rise in the room.

"Not exactly," said Miller with a half-smile. He extended his well-manicured hand in a sweeping gesture. "More like potential witnesses. We'll need your full cooperation to succeed in solving this case. Each of you must complete an affidavit confirming your whereabouts for the last twelve hours. Also, please provide any information you may think is relevant."

Gregory said, "Also, we'd like to know about any suspicious individuals you saw on your last night. Oh, and I'll need a list of anyone who recently accessed the power grid facilities."

Miller said, "One more thing. Michael Stewart,

do you have anything to say?"

Like a deer in headlights, Mike froze.

"I'm singling you out, Stewart, because we found something on Paul's workstation you need to explain."

He navigated to another file. It displayed the encrypted conversation between Mike and Paul before Wilson was killed.

Mike felt a flush creep up his neck.

Miller sighed. " The Algorithm even flagged these text messages for us. Imagine that. Nothing's secure when it's a matter of national security. And now murder."

"I was being helpful. I don't know anything beyond those text messages," Mike said, his eyes pleading for acceptance.

"Look," Amber said, "no one could imagine that Michael was involved. It was terrorists, like you said."

Mike's mind began to race. "Any clues on who they could be? How did they breach our security?"

Miller shook his head. "That's what's alarming. All logs were erased. Our only lead is an unauthorized data transfer to a foreign server. It was encrypted untraceable, but it's enough to assume that whoever did this wasn't just after Paul. They were covering tracks."

Suddenly, Mike considered the anomalies he had discovered earlier. "I think we're looking at something bigger that involves not just our facility but the Algorithm itself. It's possible that the *WormAI* attack was not just a breach, but a full-scale attack aimed to throw us off balance."

"Meaning, this could be part of a larger plan to compromise or manipulate the Algorithm," suggested Amber.

Mike added, "Paul might have also discovered it and was silenced for it."

Gault said, "If they could try to corrupt the Algorithm, that's not just a security breach. That's —"

"— potentially national security," Winters finished for him. "We need to trace that foreign server. And dive deeper into the Algorithm than any of us have ever gone."

CHAPTER 13

Deep Dive

The offices were swarming with federal agents when Mike returned the next day. They moved like bees buzzing about with stern eyes concealed behind reflective sunglasses. They perused files, inspected workstations, and disrupted the facility's workflow with an invasive vigor. They wanted to find well-hidden secrets.

And Mike had secrets to hide.

Jonah was embroiled in conversation with one of them—a hawk-nosed man with a military demeanor. The air was thick with tension and unspoken concerns. Mike's hazel eyes scanned the room, finally landing on Amber. She was visibly uneasy, hovering over her workstation as an agent audited her computer.

Mike knew he needed to talk to Jonah and Amber, but not here, not with vultures circling. He discreetly caught Amber's eye and subtly inclined his head toward the break room. She nodded almost imperceptibly.

Inside the break room, the scent of burnt coffee hung in the air. Jonah closed the door behind them, leaning against it like a barricade against an unfolding deluge.

"Status?" Jonah's voice was terse.

Mike's eyes were intense, a swirl of thoughts behind them. "I reviewed the anomalies that I mentioned to Paul."

Amber and Jonah stared at him.

"I may have found some faint signs of intrusion deep within the Algorithm. Micro-corruptions, hidden bits that don't belong. I've made copies of my findings so you can review them."

He handed each of them a flash drive.

"Foreign?" Jonah asked, his eyebrows knitting together.

"Could be. I couldn't trace it back yet; it's sophisticated, and you would know better than me."

Jonah placed the flash drive into his laptop and opened it. He and Amber looked over the files.

"Yeah. You may be right," said Jonah.

Amber said, "On top of that, I found that Paul may have been running unauthorized queries before he was killed."

Mike looked from one to the other. "So, it's true. He was looking for a mole."

Amber nodded. "It seems likely. But there's more—evidence of a planned large-scale data manipulation. This isn't just spying, or even hacking, someone is trying to pervert the Algorithm."

"That would have far-reaching consequences," Jonah said, his voice tinged with disbelief.

"We're talking about potential havoc. Financial markets collapsing, public services failing."

"And don't forget the national defense systems," Jonah interjected.

Mike felt a surge of vulnerability. His mind briefly veered off to his past—the dropout year, the aimless wandering. He had stumbled into a role of monumental responsibility, and now, with all the investigations, he felt the walls were closing in on him.

Jonah seemed to sense his internal turmoil. "Are you okay?"

Mike sighed. "Just trying to fathom the depth of the abyss we're staring into."

Jonah moved away from the door and walked over to him. "Look, you've got to hold it together. Doubt is a luxury we can't afford."

Mike met his gaze. "I know. But I can't help but wonder how I got pulled into this. And how do we even begin to fix it?"

Amber, usually so composed, seemed to struggle with her emotions. "First, we find out who's behind the murder. Mike, can you backtrace the intrusion? Identify the mole?"

"It's risky," Mike admitted. "If I dig around while the FBI is looking and get caught . . ., I'm already in the spotlight."

Amber placed her hand on his. "You're not alone

in this, Michael. We're with you."

"We'll find the mole," he said, steeling himself. "But it's going to take time."

◆ ◆ ◆

The air was thick with solemnity as Mike stood by Paul Wilson's freshly carved headstone. A picture of Paul was set on a small easel next to a wreath of white lilies. The atmosphere at the private memorial service was almost cathedral-like. Soft murmurs of condolences filled the space.

Colleagues, friends, and family gathered to honor the man whose diligence had, inadvertently, unearthed a dangerous plot. It was a ceremony of hushed voices and bowed heads. Yet each person knew that the echoes of Paul's life would reverberate much longer than the words spoken on this day.

CHAPTER 14

Downhill

Several months later, as winter approached, Mike stood on the mountain peak as dawn broke for the weekend getaway. The town below was a distant speck. The mountain cold penetrated his bones despite his MIT jacket and layered attire. He slid his fingers into thermal gloves and shifted the weight of his freshly waxed skis onto his shoulders. Each footprint he made was a crunching symphony in the snow. He went to the gondola, his heart racing as figures glided elegantly on the Massachusetts slopes.

He spotted Amber in line for the gondola and felt an electric charge.

"There you are," Mike greeted, flashing a grin that told his adrenaline-fueled anticipation.

"Couldn't stay away," Amber replied with balletic grace, gliding to his side.

An expansive panorama unfolded beneath them during the ride up. Upon reaching the advanced level platform, he snapped his goggles against his face and clicked into his skis.

He exchanged cursory hellos with a handful of familiar faces. They were all enjoying the Turing Institute's Tenth Anniversary Spring Break event. An older skier sauntered past, face chiseled by years and windburn, eyes a silent dare to match his skills. This was the crème de la crème of snow sports enthusiasts, an assembly donned in top-tier gear, poised at the brink of adrenaline-laced descents.

The skiers launched off one pair at a time until only Amber and Mike were left in splendid isolation. The mountain air tasted pure—a touch crisp.

Amber's eyes twinkled with mischief. "Race you to the bottom?"

Before Mike could question the stakes, Amber was a rocketing blaze of movement. Cursing inwardly, he thrust his poles into the snow and propelled himself after her. The skis sang—a euphoric hiss—against the powder. He leaned into the wind, feeling the resistance to his acceleration. Yet, as if commanded by some otherworldly force, Amber stayed frustratingly ahead.

With each serpentine maneuver, Mike's instincts screamed for more speed. The mountain slope was a tapestry of steep plunges, snow-choked woodlands, and skeletal trees clawing at the sky.

Taking a tuck position, he clenched his poles under his arms. The wind roared in his ears as speed blurred the details of the world passing him. Trees became spectral blurs. The very air seemed to evaporate.

Amber was tantalizingly close now, her joy echoing back at him like a taunt. Mike swept through a labyrinth of flags in a near-reckless dash, his skis carving arcane glyphs in the snow.

Then disaster.

An errant ski edge betrayed him. Time elongated, each millisecond a painting of acute chaos as he tumbled, rolled, and came to a jarring halt. He shook his head, dislodging clumps of snow.

Then, propelled by ego and the sight of Amber's diminishing figure, he sprang back up.

Ignoring the stab of warning signs that signaled an impending ravine, he shot like a bolt. Bounding over hillocks and plunging into troughs, his breathing became a rhythmic chant of exertion.

Speeding through an orchard of pines and firs, he realized the race was nearing its conclusion.

Amber was in sight, but a mere silhouette.

In a final Hail Mary, he executed a series of turns so sharp they could cut glass. Every muscle screamed in protest. And then the finish line was there, lying in ambush as if it had sprung from the snow.

Exhausted, Mike crossed it. The very act of slowing down felt like a betrayal to the adrenaline that had sustained him. His fingers remained clamped like vices around his poles; his lungs seized in their rhythmic intake of the mountain air.

Snowflakes began to fall—nature's applause for their descent.

As he finally unclamped his skis and

straightened, each movement tinged with an afterglow of ache, one thought claimed him.

Did I win?

❖ ❖ ❖

That evening, the Turing Institute's Tenth Anniversary celebration began.

Mike stepped inside the picturesque mountain chateau. Around him, the ballroom unfurled its sumptuous architecture. It was a study of rustic opulence. Chandeliers dangled like bejeweled crowns, and aged wooden furniture graced the room.

The crowd expressed the revelry and contagious cheer of the evening. Each smile, handshake, and hug were a moment knitting them together. Yet, as he scanned the faces, Mike felt invisible.

Stationed at the bar, Amber's allure caught his attention. She wore a green silk dress, a sublime fabric that seemed to melt on her skin, creating an aura rather than a mere appearance. Her golden locks were an elegant cascade vying for attention. Around her, men clustered like moths to a flame, yet her restless fingers drummed on the wooden edge of the bar, betraying an impatient yearning.

Catching the sight of Mike, her lips curled into an electrifying smile. The men around her slowly receded like the ocean tide pulling back.

"Your timing," she chuckled, "is impeccable."

"As is your beauty," Mike rejoined, "a sight for

any weary traveler."

With a glint in her eyes that mimicked the twinkle of the chandeliers above, Amber ordered a Manhattan cocktail. Mike opted for an Old-fashioned. Their glasses clinked—an audible seal to their burgeoning connection.

Romantic melodies flowed from the orchestra, each note catching the room's fragrance and turning it into sound.

The Doosan robots hustled about the room, weaving between tables and patrons serving coffee and drinks, but were ignored. Their presence was taken for granted.

Choosing a table close to the dance floor, Mike and Amber dined, feasting on the sumptuous spread and each other's words and smiles. Between forks and spoons, conversation swirled about the slopes, gossip, dreams, and quotidian ambitions. Mike found himself captivated, not just by her beauty but by her insights, which unfurled.

"You have a way of seeing things—of seeing people—that's unique," he said. "It must serve you well at work."

She looked down, modestly absorbing the compliment. "I wish it were just about observing codes and people. Talent plays a part, too."

"Which," Mike smiled, "you have in abundance."

Captured by her radiant smile, he felt a sensation far more intoxicating than any liquor could provide. Standing up, he extended his hand towards her, "Shall we dance?"

The hardwood floor of the ballroom allowed their steps to chart a movement filled with touch and sound. As her hand met the nape of his neck and her breath caressed his cheek, each fiber of his being felt her charm.

Returning to their table, they shared laughs, and continued talking.

"An unforgettable evening," Mike murmured, leaning towards her.

"It's just the beginning," she whispered, her breath touching his lips.

They stroll back to her room.

When they reached her door, she asked, "Would you like to come in for a drink?"

Her kind invitation was readily accepted.

She poured two tumblers of whiskey. "Today was glorious."

He said, "A toast."

She raised his glass. "To the victor."

He smiled, a knowing smile, and downed his drink.

She touched his arm and saw the passion in his eyes.

His arms went around her, and he kissed her long and deep.

Her body melded into his, warm and inviting.

Their lovemaking was sensual and tender.

Afterward, Amber lay naked, wrapped in his arms as they fell asleep.

CHAPTER 15

Suspicion

Two days after the anniversary celebration, Amber burst through the door into Jonah's office, her face a complex palette of dread and horror.

"What's the matter?" Jonah asked, visibly startled. "Weren't you supposed to be in the lab the entire day?"

"I was until a routine server system check revealed information about the quantum supercomputer hack."

"The *WormAI* hack?"

"Yes, that hack. And I have no idea by whom. Or at least, I think I don't."

Jonah frowned. "What does that mean?"

Amber extended her arms dramatically. "Michael's MIT jacket was stashed in a QC server farm. I have no idea how it got there. Those servers could have been the entry point for manually inserting a flash drive with executable malware."

"That attack was months ago. Do you believe Michael was behind that and is preparing for another?"

She shrugged. "I don't know, but I took the jacket."

"You didn't return it to him?"

"No."

"Where is it."

Amber dug through her bag and held the jacket at arm's length.

Jonah scrutinized it. "Apart from the MIT logo, there's no identifying mark. How can you be sure it's his?"

"He wore it skiing, and there's a note in the pocket with his name on it."

"You need to report this, Amber. Turn it over to the authorities."

"I can't. I've effectively tampered with evidence at a possible crime scene."

"But you weren't aware of that. Hold on, how could Michael even gain access to the server farm? He would have needed a special keycard to enter that facility. Where is your keycard?"

"My keycard's right here," Amber affirmed, pulling her wallet from her bag, and showing it to Jonah.

"So, what's the issue?"

Amber's face flushed a delicate pink. "He stayed in my room. He could have temporarily swiped it."

"In your room?" Jonah's eyes widened.

Amber started to pace. "What am I going to do? Call him and accuse him directly?"

"This is cybercrime. What if it's tied to Paul's death?"

"Michael's smart. He could have managed it. But what would be his motive?"

"Could he be part of some wider conspiracy? You should inform the FBI."

"I can't just throw around accusations." Amber paced more frantically now, fingers clawing through her hair. "How could he be so irresponsible losing his jacket?"

"Are you going to cover for Michael?"

"That's not what this is about."

"So, what is it about?"

"He matters to me, okay?"

Jonah sighed. "Oh, great. That makes everything so much simpler, doesn't it?"

"I don't know, Jonah. I don't know." Uncertainty nibbled at the edges of Amber's self-control.

Could Michael be involved in cybercrime, or was someone else pulling the strings?

She pushed the troubling thoughts aside.

"I need time to think," Amber finally said. "Will you give me some time?"

"I won't say anything, but you need to decide."

She tried to dismiss thoughts of Michael, the jacket, and the FBI. The ridiculousness of her situation swamped her.

She didn't get any sleep that night.

◆ ◆ ◆

Manfred Gault perused the intricate details of Michael Stewart's Digital Twin on his holographic display. His eyes narrowed as they caught a slight but deliberate edit in Stewart's timeline. Such a momentary blip that would've gone unnoticed by an untrained eye. But Gault was anything but untrained; his years in cyber-intelligence had honed his scrutiny to a keen edge.

The blip concerned a trivial period in Stewart's life, but even trivialities mattered in the Digital Twin landscape. The discrepancies in Stewart's history appeared concerning.

"Something isn't adding up," Gault muttered to himself. His fingers drummed rhythmically on his desk—each tap was a punctuated note of growing suspicion. With a swift motion, he initiated a secure call.

"Stewart, come to my office. We need to talk."

Minutes later, Mike walked in, his tall frame slightly hunched. His deep-set hazel eyes met Gault's, but not without a flicker of what might have been hesitance—or was it caution?

"Take a seat," Gault gestured, his voice crisp.

"What's this about?" Mike asked, easing into the chair.

Gault projected Stewart's Digital Twin onto the translucent screen that separated them. "Care to explain these irregularities? Especially this little modification," he pointed to the edited moment, the cursor hovering like an accusation.

Mike leaned forward, his eyes squinting at the screen. "I don't know what you're talking about," he replied, a touch of defiance in his tone.

"Let's not dance around, Stewart," Gault pressed. "Given the FBI's ongoing investigation into Paul Wilson's death and your role in our cyber-operations, any discrepancy in your background is a matter of concern."

"You think I have something to do with Paul's death?" Mike's eyes widened, but his voice remained steady, modulating between surprise and a tinge of indignation.

"I didn't say that." Gault's gaze remained level. "But let's be clear. Vague answers won't suffice. This is a crisis, and I need to know that I can trust everyone on my team."

Mike took a deep breath. "There are aspects of my life I'd rather keep private. As for trust, I've done nothing to break yours."

Gault frowned. "I hope you understand, Stewart, that a less than transparent history is a liability, not just for you, but for all of us."

"I understand," Mike said, rising from his chair. "Is there anything else?"

"No," Gault replied with evident dissatisfaction, his eyes still locked onto Mike's retreating figure. "You can go."

◆ ◆ ◆

Mike returned home, his thoughts a swirl of anxiety and concern. He came face-to-face with Michael Stewart, his expression mirroring Mike's tension.

Stewart asked, "Is something wrong?"

"We have a situation," Mike began, signing back. "Gault is becoming suspicious. He noticed my minor edit in the Digital Twin and mentioned the FBI's investigation into Paul."

Stewart looked grim. "How much does he know?"

"Enough to ask questions but not enough to connect the dots. Still, it won't be long before he might," Mike said.

"What do you propose?"

Mike hesitated. "I don't know. I need to find a way to divert suspicion without exposing us. There are greater things at stake for them to be concerned about."

"Like the Algorithm," Stewart nodded. "They can't let that slip into the wrong hands. If it becomes compromised, the consequences are unimaginable."

"Exactly," Mike affirmed. "But we can't be reckless. As Gault said, this is a time of crisis, and trust is at a premium." He paused and asked tentatively, "Perhaps we should consider running."

Stewart maneuvered his wheelchair into the center of the room. He smirked as he said, "Running?!"

"Sorry. I lost my head for a moment," said Mike, with a bleak smile. "Our identities are digitized to the point that there is no place on Earth where we can hide."

Stewart sighed, "Then we'll have to find a way to keep the trust without revealing what we're doing. But tread carefully, Mike. We're walking a very fine line."

"I'm aware," Mike said. His thoughts were heavy with the gravity of the choices ahead. Trust, after all, was a two-way street—and it was becoming increasingly unclear whom he could trust.

As he pondered, his gaze fell upon his own reflection in the darkened screen.

Who am I? Really?

The man in the mirror stared back without an answer.

CHAPTER 16

Covert Ops

In a nondescript building tucked away in the labyrinthine streets of a city far from North America, a room buzzed with low conversations. Computer blueprints and schematics adorned the walls. A real-time feed of Turing's facility was displayed on a massive screen and a team of operatives huddled beneath its glow.

At the helm was General Li, a wiry man with piercing eyes that missed no details. Flanking him were operatives Zhang and Wang—cybersecurity and field operations specialists. They were a trio of exceptional skill, a scalpel where a hammer would not suffice. And while their faces were stoic, a fire kindled in their eyes, a testament to their unyielding commitment to the mission.

Recently, China's Baidu unveiled a new generative artificial intelligence model that rivaled OpenAI's. Its effort was intended to lead the race for AI development in the world. Known as Ernie it reflected improvements in understanding, generation, logic, and memory. It formed the basis for China's newly developed Algorithm.

Li relished his work. He leaned forward, his eyes narrowing at the screen. "Cyberattacks require a lot of time and effort to create and launch. However, as AI and machine learning evolve, we have found ways to use them to develop more successful methods."

"Tell me how our efforts are paying off," he demanded, his voice laced with authority.

Cybersecurity expert Captain Zhang said quietly, "Our attack using an AI variant of *Storm Worm* was thwarted." He paused before adding, "But our new trojan is ready to masquerade as legitimate software to trick users into executing it. It's an AI variant of *Zeus*. It can bypass centralized servers and create independent servers to exploit sensitive information. We will be able to access national defense accounts and steal access codes. Then we can corrupt their quantum supercomputer mainframes, crippling their Algorithm," Zhang reported.

Li nodded then turned to his field operator leader, Major Wang.

Wang leaned over the table, pointing to a 3D holographic layout of Turing's facility. "Our ground team is in position as well. They will physically sabotage the servers to ensure maximum disruption while the cyberattack is underway."

Li gathered his thoughts for a moment, his eyes lingering on the real-time feed. He thought of his family back home, the burgeoning society that thrived under the guidance of their own brand-new Algorithm. While the world might see their work as an act of aggression, Li knew it was one of preservation. They were the guardians of a delicate equilibrium, fueled not by malice but by an unyielding duty to their nation and the AI that guided it.

"Proceed with Phase II," Li spoke the words and Zhang's fingers hit the keyboard, deploying the virus into Turing's system.

On the screen, they watched a data stream report on the code cascade, lines of corruption that would eat away at the foundation of their rival's Algorithm.

Simultaneously, Wang keyed in a command on his communication device, signaling the ground team thousands of miles away.

While the cyber assault would unfold, the operative agents on the Turing grounds had their instructions. He was confident in their abilities.

Within seconds, they received a message.

"Initial sabotage successful."

CHAPTER 17

Surgery

Inside the specialized surgical unit of Boston Medical Center, Michael Stewart lay face down on the operating table. He was covered in a sterile blue drape. The hum of machines, calibrated and powered by sophisticated AI systems, filled the room. Above him, a large holographic screen displayed a 3D image of his spine, highlighting the ruptured discs with contrasting colors.

Dr. Marylan Hayes, the lead surgeon, clad in her green surgical attire, reviewed the information on the screen. "AI System," she began, addressing the voice-activated interface. "Provide a comprehensive analysis of Mr. Stewart's spinal injuries."

The room's lighting dimmed slightly as the AI system, named AURA, projected a holographic diagnostic report into the air.

Patient: Michael Stewart.

Diagnosis: Two ruptured lumbar discs—L4 L5.

Recommended procedure: minimally invasive AI-assisted spinal fusion.

Michael tried to remain calm, his breaths slow and deliberate. He had researched the procedure, yet the thought of machines working inside him was still unnerving.

"Will I feel anything?" he asked, his voice shaky.

Dr. Hayes reassured him, "You'll be under local anesthesia. The procedure is minimally invasive, and AURA's precision is unparalleled. You won't feel anything other than pressure against your body."

A robotic arm, with a series of delicate instruments attached, positioned itself over Michael's lower back. Dr. Hayes began the operation.

"AURA, initiate lumbar access."

Guided by the AI's intricate algorithms, the robot made a tiny incision.

"Deploy nanobots," ordered Dr. Hayes.

The AI-assisted procedure utilized nanobots. They would minimize the surgical opening and potential muscle damage. Once inside, these microscopic robots provided real-time feedback to AURA. It aided in precision and minimized error.

The nanobots' primary function was to clear the area around the ruptured discs. They removed any debris or fragmented disc material. Their microscopic size allowed for unparalleled accuracy. As they worked, another set of nanobots synthesized a biocompatible material. Making it ready to replace the damaged disc segments.

"Preparing for spinal fusion," Dr. Hayes declared.

With the area cleared, AURA guided the robotic arm to introduce the synthesized material. This cushion between the vertebrae mimicked the natural disc's function while promoting bone growth, thus fusing the vertebrae over time.

Michael, conscious yet feeling no pain, heard the doctors' orders and AURA's periodic status updates. It was surreal knowing that machines and AI were reshaping his spine.

Once the fusion material was in place, the nanobots facilitated the final phase, initiating the healing process. They released a combination of growth factors and stem cells to expedite tissue repair and reduce inflammation.

"Procedure complete," announced AURA, its voice neutral yet somehow reassuring. The screen above displayed a before-and-after image of Michael's spine.

Dr. Hayes sighed in relief. "Everything went perfectly, Michael. Now for the recovery."

She added, "The recovery plan was powered by the same AI technology. For six weeks, you'll wear an exoskeleton during your waking hours. AURA will calibrate it to provide support while allowing limited movement. This promotes healing without putting strain on the fused area."

Michael looked intrigued. "And after?"

"Post the initial recovery, AURA will design a personalized physical therapy program. It'll use augmented reality to guide you through exercises, ensuring you regain strength and flexibility. This combination of traditional therapy and AI insights ensures optimal recovery."

The concept of melding technology and the human touch fascinated Michael. "So, I'm in the hands of machines?"

"Not just machines. A collaboration of human expertise and AI precision." Hayes chuckled. "You're in good hands, Michael."

In the days that followed Michael's surgery, he experienced the marvels of modern medicine. Though a bit daunting at first, the exoskeleton soon became second nature. It provided support and stability. Yet, its AI-driven adaptability meant he could perform everyday tasks with minimal discomfort.

The augmented reality therapy sessions would require six weeks. They were equally groundbreaking. Michael would put on AR glasses, immersing him in a virtual world. He would perform exercises that mimicked real-world activities guided by AURA. It provided a safe environment to push boundaries without the risk of injury.

He waited patiently for Mike's visit.

CHAPTER 18

Deus Ex Machina

Mike sat at his workstation in Turing's Digital Command Center, staring intently at the screen. His fingers twitched above the keyboard, hesitating. The programs running on the Turing servers were acting erratically. They were sending out alarm bells across various diagnostics tests—a breach.

Jonah sat across from Mike in the war room deep within the Turing facility. The room was dimly lit, the tension palpable as they stared at the myriad screens. Yet, Jonah's faith in his friend was uncertain.

Jonah asked, "Michael, what's happening? Systems are going haywire."

Mike sighed. "We're under attack. A trojan has infiltrated the mainframe masquerading as a legitimate microservice. An AI controller is coordinating botnet attacks and evading takedowns. The distributed botnet is robust and adaptive. It's trying to disable the Algorithm through corrupting its routine microservices."

Jonah sounded an institution-wide alert.

Mike felt a tight knot form in his stomach. "It's not just disabling it. It's also downloading confidential files to an unknown server. This is beyond just messing with our Algorithm."

Jonah's eyes widened. "That's espionage, not mere hacking. Do you have any clue who's behind it?"

"No," Mike confessed, "but we need to stop it before it escalates."

Amber's face popped onto his screen. "Michael, I got your message. How bad is it?"

"Bad," he replied curtly. "If we can't contain this in time, we're looking at Algorithm design secrets being stolen."

Amber grimaced. "I've alerted security. But Michael, remember you still haven't been cleared of Paul's death. Be careful how you handle this."

Mike clenched his fists, feeling cornered. Here he was, fighting off a cyber espionage attack while under suspicion for a crime he didn't commit. And Gault was nosing into his ID background as well. The irony wasn't lost on him. But how could he worry about clearing his name when so much was threatened?

Jonah sensed his concern. "Look, you're the genius who scored high on the career exam. You've got to solve this puzzle and keep the Algorithm safe. That's your job as an Assistant Keeper."

Mike dived into lines of code, wrestling with

the malicious virus that slithered through Turing's digital veins. Sweat trickled down his forehead as he navigated the intricate coding. He tried to isolate the virus and prevent the download of sensitive files.

He couldn't help but wonder who could engineer such a sophisticated attack. This was not the work of a criminal hacker organization. It was coordinated, calculated, and lethal. And it bore the fingerprints of a state-backed operation.

While part of his brain unraveled the intricate coding of the virus, another part sifted through the questions about Paul's death. Was it connected to this breach? And did the clues that seemed to point to him serve as a smokescreen for something far more nefarious?

Finally, he isolated a string of code that seemed to be the heart of the virus.

Mike said, "It seems they're employing an extremely complex and adaptive algorithm. They're not just looking to disrupt but to corrupt and decimate our system."

His eyes widened as he realized the extent of its sophisticated, tight code. Whoever wrote this had an intimate knowledge of Turing's architecture and a deep understanding of AI systems.

He initiated a scan to find the trojan bots and put them into a caged sandbox. Sweat dripped onto his keyboard as the progress bar slowly inched forward.

80%.
90%.
98%.

A chime rang out, signaling that the virus had been contained. But Mike knew it was only temporary. He sat back, exhaling a breath he didn't know he was holding.

"The virus is contained," he informed Amber and Jonah.

Amber let out a sigh of relief. "Good job. But now, we must find out who did this—and if it's connected to Paul's death."

Mike looked at their faces. Here he was, sandwiched between protecting the Algorithm and protecting his identity.

◆ ◆ ◆

Jacob Winters called his cybersecurity team to the Escher conference room for a briefing. The atmosphere was thick with anticipation. The Keeper of the Algorithm had never faced a challenge quite like this. But then again, the Algorithm had never been so threatened.

"In the last few hours, new and more potent cyberattacks have been perpetrated," said Winters.

Reports flashed across their screens showing the level the cyberattacks had reached. They were penetrating Turing's critical infrastructure. The power grids, servers, and basic systems were in disarray.

"I am forming an action team to find the source. Manfred Gault, as Associate Keeper of R&D, you'll be the point man. Your role will be to coordinate our efforts," said Winters, nodding at Gault.

He turned and said, "Michael Stewart, given your unique skills and role in bringing the suspect anomalies to light, you'll lead the code investigation."

He then glanced at Jonah, whose screen was filled with cybersecurity frameworks and firewalls. "Jonah Jenson, your data analysis expertise is vital. You'll be working in tandem with Stewart. Your task is to dig deep into our system vulnerabilities and help us fortify our defenses."

Finally, his eyes landed on Amber Hearst, who sat poised and attentive. "Amber, you're my eyes and ears. As my special assistant, you'll act as the liaison between this team and me. Keep me abreast of all significant developments. Time is of the essence. We must find out who's behind the hacks, how they're pulling them off, and neutralize the threat—immediately."

Gault leaned forward and said, his voice tinged with anger, "This is no longer a game of cat and mouse. We're facing actions that transcend cyber."

The team felt the urgency escalate like a tinderbox catching fire. They went about their assignments. And as they plunged back into their screens, data streams, and lines of code, each knew they were not just Keepers. They were the last line of defense.

◆ ◆ ◆

General Li felt a momentary exhilaration of

triumph, quickly suppressed. There was no room for emotion, only the completion of the mission.

He waited for news of the operation's success. But instead, a message flashed on the screen, an anomaly they had not predicted.

"Turing countermeasures have been initiated," reported Zhang. "Turing cybersecurity has partially contained our trojan."

Li's eyes narrowed. "What's happening now?"

" It seems they've detected the intrusion. They've successfully isolated part of their system. We did not expect such a swift reaction," Zhang said, his voice mingled with disbelief.

Li thought of the faceless adversary who had fought off their virus, an enemy as unseen as they were. For the first time, he felt a flicker of doubt. Were they underestimating the capabilities of Turing's guardians?

"What about the physical attacks on the Institute's infrastructure?"

"They are much more successful. Our agents are continuing to make progress."

"Adjust plans. I want contingencies in place," Li ordered, erasing any trace of emotion from his voice. There was no room for doubt, only action.

His operators nodded. They turned back to their stations to evaluate new strategies. They were already formulating another wave of attack, another infiltration vector.

Li couldn't shake off a newfound respect for their adversary as they worked. They were no longer faceless objects. They were a worthy opponent. And while this realization did not waver his commitment to his duty, it fanned the flames of the fire that burned within him.

But even in that moment of reluctant admiration, Li knew it would not alter his mission. His commitment was to his country, to his own Algorithm. In this war of zeroes and ones, the lines were blurred. Alliances unsteady.

And as Li looked at his team, their faces were a mosaic of concentration and resolve. He knew they were bound by something more significant than personal ambition or curiosity. They were bound by duty. And it was a bond that would not, could not, be broken.

But one thing was clear—there was no room for failure because covert operatives who failed tended to disappear.

◆ ◆ ◆

Mike spoke up, "I've identified potential backdoors in our own system. I'm working on sealing it now. And we need to trace the source of these hacks. If we can do that, we can predict their next move."

Amber looked equally focused. "I'll inform Winters. We need to coordinate a multi-faceted response. We may use our diplomatic channels to defuse the political overtones while countering the cyber offensive."

As they all nodded, the room reverberated with

a new kind of tension—a fusion of determination and hope.

"Ready?" Mike's voice was almost a whisper as if he feared the walls themselves were listening.

"Ready as I'll ever be," Jonah replied, his tone subdued.

Mike's fingers tapped out new code as he navigated through the layers of cybersecurity. The digital walls of the offshore server crumbled under the assault of his expertise. His eyes never wavered from the screen.

Soon, Mike broke through. On the screen appeared an interface, dissimilar from Turing's own, distinctly foreign.

Jonah leaned in closer, his eyes narrowing. "What am I looking at? Are we in?"

"We're in," said Mike. "I've located the source of the enemy attack. It's an AI operation remote based outside of Beijing, China."

Mike scrolled through screens and executed commands. "And not just any operation—this is advanced, way beyond what we've seen before. They're not just trying to manipulate the Algorithm. They're creating a counterpart. An antithesis Algorithm of their own."

Jonah was silent, taking a moment to digest Mike's words. "You're saying they can steal enough information from our Algorithm, to create their own Chinese Algorithm?"

Mike nodded. "Exactly. They've been siphoning data, reverse-engineering key modules, and now they're near completion of their own version."

Jonah felt a shiver crawl up his spine. His skepticism was eroding. In its place, a newfound loyalty toward Mike began to build.

"So, what's our move?"

Mike looked away from the screen and locked eyes with Jonah. "First, we gather as much intelligence as we can. Then, we prepare for cyberwar."

Mike resumed his keyboard work. Jonah watched. His earlier reservations about Mike's capabilities or role in this digital maze were gone.

Suddenly, a red flash erupted on the screen, and a digital siren warned of unauthorized activity. Mike's fingers froze mid-air, his eyes widening.

"Damn it, they've detected us," he murmured, his voice mingled with disbelief and concern.

The screen went black momentarily then a message appeared in bold, red letters:

ACCESS TERMINATED!

Mike sighed, frustrated. "We've been booted, and they've probably traced us back to Turing. This might accelerate their plans."

Jonah felt a surge of anxiety but forced it back down. "Then we accelerate ours."

Both men sat there, the weight of their newfound knowledge pressing down upon them like an unseen hand. The room seemed darker, reflecting the murky waters they had just waded into.

"Jonah," Mike spoke softly, contemplating each word, "I need to know you're with me. Because things are about to get very complicated, very fast."

Jonah looked at Mike, his eyes meeting those deep-set pools of complexity and resolve. And in that moment, any remnants of skepticism shattered, leaving only a steadfast commitment.

"I'm with you," he said, his voice unwavering. "And I think we have some important news to tell Amber."

CHAPTER 19

Shadow

Amber sat in her compact, dimly lit office, surrounded by monitors that cast a soft, bluish glow. She had been sifting through lines of code for hours, her eyes bleary but focused. Mike had contained the virus in a caged sandbox, but containment was not eradication. She felt it was up to her to help identify, dissect, and neutralize the rogue software.

Her heart, though, was a complex maze of emotions. Mike, whom she cared about, was still a suspect in an investigation.

Can I trust him?

For now, she had to put her feelings in a lockbox and bury it deep within her.

Her fingers hit the keys, entering commands, and trying to eliminate all traces of the enemy virus. She launched a forensic tool designed to analyze malware. It scanned through the complexities of the virus and dissected its DNA.

As the software worked, her mind drifted to Manfred Gault. They had dated for several months. Then, the weekend in the mountains with Mike changed everything. She could tell that Gault sensed the difference.

I don't know what I want.

The screen blinked. The results were in. Amber's eyes widened. The malware was coded with intricate multi-layered encryption techniques that were cutting-edge.

She initiated a countermeasure protocol, a digital antibody to neutralize the virus. Her fingers hesitated for a moment before hitting the 'Enter' key.

What if Mike had something to do with this?
Could she be unwittingly helping him?
Duty wrestled with emotion.
She pressed the key.

The countermeasures navigated the labyrinthine architecture of Turing's systems. It deployed antibots to prevent any reinfection. Amber watched, her eyes tracking every movement and every process, waiting for some sign of success or failure.

A notification popped up on her screen. Her countermeasures were complete. She exhaled, feeling a strange mix of relief and apprehension.

Her internal comm buzzed, and Jonah's face appeared on her screen. "Amber, any progress?"

"It's done," she said, her voice tinged with exhaustion. "I wrote a Python patch to our cybersecurity software. It will hunt down and delete any more of this malicious package. The countermeasures will do their job."

Jonah nodded. "Good. You and Michael are proving to be quite the dynamic duo. He was able to track the source to a lab in China. We got lots of info."

Amber said, "We might have this thing beat for now, but we can never be sure we get every bot. There's always one that will hide in the weeds to come bursting out later."

The mention of Mike stirred something in her. "Jonah, do you trust Michael?"

Jonah sighed. "I've known him long enough to know he's got integrity. But he's also caught in a web of circumstances. So, to answer your question, yeah, I kinda trust him. But I also know we need evidence to clear him."

Amber nodded, her mind grappling with her friend's words. She, too, wanted to believe in Mike, but she couldn't let that cloud her judgment.

As she waited for the final report from her countermeasure program, Amber found her mind drifting back to her first meeting with Mike. His awkward charm, undeniable intelligence, and deep hazel eyes seemed to look right into her soul. She had fallen for him then, and she had fallen hard. But life had thrown them into a tangle of ethical and emotional issues that neither had anticipated.

The computer beeped, snapping her out of her reverie. Her countermeasures were in place against any future intrusion. A wave of relief washed over her, but it was short-lived. Now came the hard part—finding out who was behind this and how it connected to Paul's murder.

She contacted Mike and Jonah. "It's done. The virus has been neutralized in the Turing facilities. I sent the antidote to the infected infrastructure computers, but it will take time to cure them."

Mike's face showed a mixture of relief and concern. "Thank you, Amber. You've done well."

Amber felt a need for professional detachment as she looked into his eyes. She was walking a tightrope with a shadow of doubt.

CHAPTER 20

Crunch

Mike watched the steering wheel as the AI autopilot navigated the rugged dirt road that led away from the Turing Institute. The car's headlights illuminated an unassuming building in the distance, and Mike couldn't help but sigh in recognition.

"This is the place," he murmured. He glanced sideways at Amber, whose foot tapped rhythmically against the car floor in evident nervousness.

Amber said, "Seems like an unlikely spot for a data server farm. Who would think of looking here for evidence of infiltration? But, if one were planning a covert op against the Turing system, this place is ideal."

Her gaze met Mikes, questions swirling behind her eyes. The unspoken query about his MIT jacket hung in the air.

The AI parked the car in front of the building.

They exited the car. A gust of cold air greeted them. Amber's access key card granted them entrance to the building. The vast interior was an infinite maze of servers, and the loud hum of electronics filled the space. Methodically, Amber set up her laptop, murmuring, "I'll begin the diagnostic."

As she worked, a soft shuffling echoed from a darker corner of the room. Mike's head whipped around, his voice barely above a whisper. "Did you hear that?"

Before Amber could respond, a figure lunged from the shadows. Mike reacted instantly, deflecting the assault, and landing a swift punch that knocked out his opponent.

No sooner had he done so than a second assailant targeted Amber, his blade glinting menacingly in the dim light. In a graceful evasion, Amber narrowly avoided the blade's bite.

But their brief respite ended abruptly. The unmistakable slam of car doors outside echoed ominously. Two more figures burst into the room, their expressions a canvas of savage intent. The sheer size of one was imposing, a scar marring his face. His companion, though smaller, moved with a wiry intensity.

Mike's voice shouted out. "Amber!"

Without hesitation, she grabbed the keyboard. Swinging it with all her might, her attacker went down, stunned.

Mike grappled with his own foe, a mix of punches, dodges, and tackles, each trying to overpower the other in a battle of will and strength.

Amber screamed, "Mike, get down!"

He dropped as a bullet whizzed past him, hitting a nearby wall. Splinters exploded.

Mike took a deep breath. In a burst of speed that caught his opponent off guard, Mike lunged forward. Blow for blow, he managed to topple the hulking brute, pinning him with a determination born of adrenaline and fear. His fists met flesh. It was a straight punch to the man's gut, followed by an uppercut that connected with his jaw. The assailant staggered; his eyes filled with disbelief.

Seizing the moment of his opponent's disorientation, Mike used his leg to sweep the man off his feet.

"Run!" Mike yelled. Amber snatched her laptop and sprinted towards the exit. Hot on her heels, Mike shut the door as they burst out of the building.

The attackers slammed out of the door.

Mike and Amber's hearts pounded like frenzied drumbeats as they scrambled into their car. Mike thrust the key into the ignition and took manual control. The engine roared to life. With a surge of power, they sped off, leaving a cloud of dust and gravel in their wake.

"Headlights," Amber murmured, her voice filled with worry. She watched the flickering lights grow in the rearview mirror.

"They're coming," Amber declared as she called for help on her cell phone.

Mike gritted his teeth, his grip tightening on the

wheel. "Hold on, this is going to be wild." His hands moved across the controls, bringing his AI into action while guiding the car over the rugged roads.

Mike glanced at Amber. "This is bigger than we thought. We're not just fighting algorithms and codes but fighting terrorists in the real world."

The chaser was relentless. Their headlights had a menacing glow as they gained ground despite Mike's evasive maneuvers across the vacant field.

"They're good," he muttered.

He felt the force of acceleration as he swerved and weaved, trying to shake off their tail. His eyes flickered, scanning for any obstacle that might thwart his path. Despite the high-speed ballet of physics and mechanics, their pursuer was closing in.

"Damn!" Mike cursed as he saw the other car roar closer through his peripheral vision. Realizing his error too late, he found himself on a perilous mountain stretch of road—his AI voice broke through the tension like a clap of thunder.

> "TOO CLOSE. AVOID."

> "BRACE FOR IMPACT!"

"Mike!" Amber screamed, her voice full of fear and urgency.

> "TOO CLOSE. AVOID."

> "BRACE FOR IMPACT!"

The sound pierced through Mike's disorientation, clearing his mind. He couldn't fail now. Not when so much was at stake.

Mike twisted the wheel desperately. He transformed what could have been a fatal crash into a semi-controlled catastrophe.

Both cars skidded off the road with a screeching of tires and a discordant symphony of metal and glass. They crashed into the mountain side.

When the world stopped spinning, Mike was disoriented amid the smoke and wreckage. Gasping through the acrid air, he unfastened his seatbelt, staggered out of the vehicle. Then he helped Amber.

He scrambled back with a newfound resolve, as he locked eyes with the assailants struggling to climb out of their destroyed vehicle.

But before anyone could act, sirens closed in.

FBI agents and police swarmed the scene.

The attackers were led away in handcuffs. Their pockets were filled with hacking tools and high-level clearance codes

◆ ◆ ◆

Jonah stared through the one-way glass into the FBI interrogation room. On the other side sat the enemy agents disarmed and bound, but still radiating an aura of dangerous intent. They fascinated him—their unwavering eyes and disciplined posture. They threatened the existence of his world, and perhaps even the world at large.

FBI agent Miller walked in, a folder of documents in his hand. "Preliminary interrogations have given us something to work with," he said, his voice tinged with grim urgency.

Jonah had front-row seats behind the one-way glass to observe the interrogation.

Miller glared at the enemy. "It's not just about the Algorithm. There's something bigger at play. You intended to instigate international conflict."

Jonah felt a jolt run through him. The words rang in his ears.

Miller said, "We have enough to be concerned, not enough to be certain. But given what you were willing to do here, we take the threat very seriously."

Jonah stared at the spies, his thoughts swirling in confusion and anger. What he once considered an act of duty was now unfolding. It threatened to upend the very foundation of civilization. His long-standing beliefs about technology's role as a neutral tool were shattering.

"So, is it true?" Miller asked, staring at the spies. "Were you planning to plunge the Institute into chaos?"

One of them—a man with steely eyes—spoke up, "We're not the ones setting the world on fire. We're just following orders."

"By provoking strife? By risking lives?"

"By doing our duty," he shot back.

"Your duty to what? To whom? To a country that doesn't understand the human cost of its actions, or to a cause that doesn't consider the consequences?"

The spies remained silent, but their eyes spoke volumes.

Jonah thought of Mike and Amber, then returned to look at the spies behind the one-way glass.

◆ ◆ ◆

The next day, Johan stood outside the facility, watching black SUVs roll through the gates. Their windows were tinted to conceal the identities of those inside. The captured Chinese agents were being transferred into the custody of federal authorities. Their faces were grim and unreadable as they were led away.

However, the investigation into Paul Wilson's death had come to an end. Mike was officially cleared because the actual murderers confessed.

The evening news carried a story about the thwarting of an international incident.

CHAPTER 21

Healing

The ambulance drove Amber and Mike to the hospital after the car crash. In the emergency clinic, a nurse greeted them and signed them in. They were led to separate treatment rooms and immediately given CAT scans and blood tests.

The nurse bustled about the rooms, prepping them for treatment with an antiseptic spray and draping them in a sterile cloth. Then, she administered an analgesic and set out the tools for the doctor's treatment. One doctor examined Mike's injured arm and shoulder, while another treated Amber's internal injuries.

"Tsk, tsk, you need significant care," she said, shaking her head in disgust as she stitched Mike's injuries. "This is a serious wound, although the onsite treatment looks quite competent."

Mike nodded as the doctor began looking over the wounds. With his injuries numbed, he watched as the surgeon peeled away the damaged skin with the help of AI-directed auto-surgery. Then, she grafted on collagen and a new skin based on his stem cells.

After an hour, the nurse bandaged the repairs, the doctor smiled. "A perfect job if I do say so myself. Though if you had had genetic enhancements, your stem cells would have produced a cleaner match."

"Do you see many genetically enhanced people?" asked Mike.

"Well, that's a complicated question." The doctor paused.

"Are the genetic enhancements pretty much the same for everyone?" asked Mike.

"Oh, no," said the doctor. "Everyone's DNA is unique, except for twins, of course. So, each DNA enhancement is a custom job. The doctor takes the DNA from the father—the sperm donor—and fertilizes an egg from his female partner. The DNA of the resulting embryo is then extracted and chemically altered by removing diseased or disadvantaged genes. Then, favorable enzyme and hormone production genes are turned on. The fertilized embryo is then implanted in the mother's womb, and she carries the baby to term. The results are often good, but not perfect."

The doctor concluded, "You can remove the bandages in three weeks. You should have virtually no scars. The results will be invisible to the eye."

Once he was feeling better and able to walk, Mike went to see Amber. Instead of a sterile hospital room full of tubes and instruments, her room looked like it might have been transplanted from her home. It was complete with holographs of personal items and photos of her family. Soothing music played quietly in the background. Unobtrusive monitors under her bed informed the nursing station of her condition.

Mike was relieved to find her sitting up in bed. She was still groggy from the medications and took a few minutes to recognize him, but when she did, she reached out a hand toward him and said, "Michael! You're all right!"

"Fine. How are you?"

"Much better. They tell me it'll take time, but I'll make a full recovery."

Amber's eyes hinted at a depth of pain and weariness. Mike could see the faint trace of blue around her lips. There was an almost imperceptible flinch when she shifted in bed. These were telltale signs that her injuries were more than skin deep.

Dr. Johnson, with a holographic tablet in hand, approached Mike. "Amber's situation is a bit complex," he began, his tone measured but reassuring. "While the external injuries will heal well, we've identified internal trauma—a splenic rupture, to be precise. It's causing internal bleeding, and we need to address it immediately.

Mike's heart sank. "What does the procedure entail?"

Dr. Jensen tapped on his tablet, and a 3D model of Amber's spleen appeared, with the damaged areas highlighted. "Fortunately, we have the latest AI-assisted medical technology at our disposal.

Traditionally, this would require open surgery. But our AI-assisted nanobots can be introduced into her bloodstream. These nanobots are designed to locate the rupture and release clotting agents. They would stem the bleeding while mending the damaged tissue."

Mike looked at the detailed projection, amazed at how far medical technology had advanced. "How long will this take?"

"The procedure takes only an hour," Dr. Johnson explained. "But complete recovery will take several weeks. The nanobots will remain in her system for a few days to ensure everything is healing correctly. Afterward, they'll biodegrade harmlessly."

Mike's brow furrowed with worry. "And after? What's the recovery plan?"

The doctor's eyes softened, understanding the depth of Mike's concern. "Post-procedure, Amber will need physiotherapy. The trauma from the accident, combined with the internal injuries, means her body will need to retrain certain movements. Our AI will customize a rehabilitation program for her. It will use virtual reality to simulate everyday activities, helping her regain strength and confidence."

The doctor continued, "But physical healing is just one aspect. Car accidents can leave emotional scars, often deeper and more persistent than physical ones. Our hospital offers a unique form of therapy using augmented reality. Patients are immersed in a calm and familiar environment. It helps reduce anxiety and PTSD symptoms."

Mike nodded, absorbing the information. "I want the best for her. Whatever it takes."

Dr. Johnson smiled warmly. "She's in good hands. Our AI system has a success rate of 99.99% in similar cases. And with the combined efforts of our dedicated medical team, Amber has every chance of making a full recovery within a few weeks."

◆ ◆ ◆

During the next few days, Mike witnessed the marvel of medical science. Every day, Amber made progress. The nanobots worked wonders, mending her internal injuries with precision. The VR-assisted physiotherapy sessions, although challenging, gradually improved her mobility. Amber often pushed past her limits with her indomitable spirit, determined to get back on her feet.

Mike often joined her during the AR therapy sessions. The system created serene environments—lush green meadows, tranquil beaches, majestic mountains—places that held meaning for Amber. They would sit, talk, and sometimes enjoy the simulated sunset, finding comfort in each other's company.

However, the healing process was long and tedious. One afternoon, when Amber was looking particularly melancholy, Mike realized she needed a little cheer.

So, with a great big grin, he volunteered, "Yesterday, I asked DeepMind, 'Why aliens haven't visited our planet?'"

"I'll bite," Amber replied with a smirk. "What was his answer?"

"Terrible ratings. One star."

They laughed hysterically, pretending it was the funniest thing they had ever heard.

CHAPTER 22

♦ ♦ ♦

A month had passed since the car crash, and amid the elegant steel and glass façade of the Turing Institute, urgent chimes sounded once more. It was the frantic alert of a full-blown cyber crisis.

Mike sat before a sprawling array of monitors in the Digital Command Center. His eyes, usually lost in thought, now flashed with grim determination. By his side was Amber. She had only recently returned to work, and now she was attempting to decipher the root of the problem.

"Amber, they've done it again. It's another worm variant. But it's not just any worm—it's multiplying exponentially, sending copies of itself, and burrowing deeper into the country's financial networks," Mike declared.

Amber's face was pale as she analyzed the

code. "It's a polymorphic worm, Michael. Every time it replicates, it alters its signature. Standard firewalls can't detect it. This is sophisticated stuff. And this time, it's not just Turing that's infected. This is nationwide."

The Institute buzzed with frantic energy, echoing the digital chaos it had battled before. As Mike scrolled through the anomaly reports, he noted the breach points. Wall Street servers, federal reserves, and even cryptocurrency networks were being hit. The financial backbone of North America was under siege.

"Amber, our biggest vulnerability is the interconnectedness of it all. The worm can hop from a small-scale broker in Vancouver, feed on its data, then tunnel its way to a banking giant in New York."

She nodded. "And with the increasing push for digital currencies, the danger is even more acute. Without tangible assets to back trades, an advanced worm could create artificial inflation, or worse, hyperinflation."

Mike said, "This virus AI is optimizing viral cryptocurrency mining operations across infected hosts."

Amber paused, an idea forming. "But, Mike, if it replicates, it must leave a trace—a breadcrumb of its path. What if we develop a counter AI algorithm? Track its replication patterns, predict its next move, and corner it."

Mike's gaze sharpened. "Yes, a digital snare. Force it to reveal itself. But to execute it, we'd need vast computational resources."

A thought occurred to him . . . *the Algorithm*.

Could it be the key? Could they harness their immense power to save the financial network?

"Amber," he whispered, "we need to employ the Algorithm. It's the most advanced machine learning model on the planet. It is directly connected to all types of financial transactions, from credit cards, loans, stock, and transferring money. If anything can predict and corner this financial worm, it's the Algorithm."

Amber hesitated. "The Algorithm, with all its power, is also unpredictable. Michael, we don't fully understand it. What if we unleash something even more uncontrollable?"

Mike looked into Amber's concerned eyes, understanding her hesitation. "I know the risks but look at the stakes. The very foundation of our economy is crumbling. Trillions of dollars could be lost."

With a deep breath, Amber nodded. "Let's go to Gault and get authorization."

"We should go directly to Winters."

"Gault will be furious if we bypass him."

"There's no time to waste. We can send him a message on our way to see Winters."

Amber knew there would be repercussions but nodded anyway.

They went to Winters and began explaining their plan. Soon, the office overflowed with specialists and Associate Keepers all offering their opinion. Gault was the most obstreperous.

Gault said, "We resolved the *WormAI* without using the Algorithm."

"The *WormAI* was restricted to the Turing Institute. This is a nationwide attack that is morphing into a broader threat," said Amber.

"The Algorithm is the perfect antivirus software tool to deal with this. It is nearly universally distributed, extremely fast, and accurate," said Mike.

Gault said, "Alterations to the Algorithm must be strictly controlled. The type of changes you propose will unleash untold consequences. We wouldn't know what the results would be over time."

Mike said, "Nevertheless, the damage being done will reach catastrophic dimensions in mere hours."

It took more than two hours before a small change to the Algorithm was authorized. Mike hoped it would be enough.

The Turing Institute became the epicenter of a silent battle. Mike, Amber, and the team funneled the worm's data into the Algorithm, feeding it patterns, vulnerabilities, and behaviors.

The Algorithm created its own cybersecurity subroutine aptly named *Sentinel*. The *Sentinel* scanned billions of files per second and processed them faster than ever. It emitted money solutions, strategies, and countermeasures. It suggested isolating financial databases, rerouting stock trades, and even freezing certain assets momentarily.

The *Sentinel* operated as a guardian, detecting

each new instance of the worm, and before it could further replicate, it would trap and erase it. In parallel, a series of firebreaks were established. A digital partitioning of North America's financial networks prevented further penetration.

After a full day, Mike watched in silent awe as the last traces of the worm were found, captured, and destroyed by the Algorithm's tool, *Sentinel*.

The immediate financial crisis had been averted, but the implications were clear. The financial systems had vulnerabilities.

"The world was on the brink, Amber. And it was technology that both imperiled and saved it," said Mike.

She leaned into him, seeking comfort in their shared ordeal. "Michael, it's not technology but how it is used. We need to be prepared. This is just the beginning."

◆ ◆ ◆

Mike leaned against the bar counter, watching Amber walk through the entrance. She looked fine. A gentle melody played in the background, creating a cozy ambiance in the otherwise lively restaurant.

Amber's eyes met Mike's. She smiled and made her way toward him.

"You look amazing," Mike said.

"You're not so bad yourself," she replied, her eyes shining with genuine warmth.

They went to a quiet corner table tucked away

from the bustle. Mike held out the chair for her, and she sat down gracefully. Once seated, he reached across the table to take her hand. She looked at him, her eyes softening.

"I've been looking forward to tonight," he said. "I need a break after the last few days."

"Me too," she replied. "This should be a nice change."

Mike said, "You know, all this work—it's so easy to lose ourselves. It's moments like this, sitting across from you, that make it worthwhile."

Amber smiled, her eyes softening. "I feel the same way, Michael.

The waiter came by to take their dinner orders, and as he walked away, Mike felt his phone buzz. A message from Jonah. "Team meeting tomorrow. Urgent."

He frowned.

A few minutes later, his phone buzzed again. He glanced at the screen—it was Gault. "Come to headquarters. Now. Urgent matter."

His frown turned into a scowl. "I'm sorry, Amber. I must go. Something's up."

Her eyes met his. "It's okay, Michael. I understand."

Amber looked at her half-eaten meal, then back at Mike. "I guess our lives are too complicated for a normal date night, huh?"

Mike chuckled, "In our line of work, what's normal anyway?"

He leaned in and gave her a gentle kiss.

They got up, and he helped her into her coat. His lips brushing against hers, a simple yet intimate gesture.

"I promise we'll finish this date properly next time," he said.

"I'll hold you to that," she replied.

❖ ❖ ❖

Gault was sitting at his desk when Mike rushed into the Turing team's headquarters. His eyes were on his laptop screen.

"Is everything alright?" Mike asked.

Gault sat behind his desk his eyes fixed on his computer screen. On it was a dossier—Mike's history, or at least what he could find. Several pieces didn't add up, loose threads in an otherwise ordinary record.

Gault's eyes narrowed. "Sit down. We have a situation that requires immediate attention. The rest can wait."

Mike listened to Gault detail the cyber threat information they had recently intercepted. But after several minutes of discussion, it seemed unimportant. Mike couldn't shake the feeling that this sudden meeting was Gault's way of asserting control, of reminding him that he was still a subordinate.

After Mike left, Gault opened a secure line. He ordered his security chief, "Dig deeper into Stewart's background . . . college years, work history, everything. Something doesn't feel right. I want to know what he's hiding."

"Understood," came the terse reply before the line went dead.

Gault leaned back in his chair, his eyes narrowing. Mike had been too unusual, too talented. It was as if he'd been groomed for this assignment, which didn't sit well with him.

There were ripples in the data stream. They were minor but noticeable, and Gault was keen on finding the stone that caused them.

CHAPTER 23

Silk Road

General Li sat rigidly in his chair, staring at the encrypted message flashing on his computer screen. The corners of his lips tightened.

"Send in the team," he ordered into the intercom.

Three officers filed into the office. Its sterile atmosphere was intensified by large computer screens displaying maps detailing American vulnerabilities.

The officers stood at attention, awaiting his direction.

"High command has issued new orders," began General Li. "In light of China's digital Silk Road, we intend to rewire the world and reshape the world order. Our mission is to become the world's chief network operator and reap a commercial and strategic windfall. We will retool the global data flows, finance, and communications using Huawei's chips."

Li was aware that China's satellites had become the surveillance eyes to monitor its population and maintain social control. The government claimed it was necessary to maintain national security and social order. Naturally, Li supported these methods because he was dedicated to the State. It would never occur to him to challenge his orders.

Locking eyes with each subordinate, Li said, "We are transitioning to Phase Three. I want your thoughts."

Captain Zhang hesitated before speaking. "Sir, the Americans have already traced these cyberattacks back to our lab once. They might do so again. They could counterattack this lab directly."

Li turned to the screen, displaying their intrusion vectors concealed through layers of proxy servers. "We've been meticulous and have constructed secure defenses. But even if they do strike, we will be well on the way to achieving the 'probabilistic advantage.'"

"Probabilistic advantage, sir?" asked Lieutenant Chu, her brows furrowing.

Li sighed. "It's the point where their nuclear deterrence is so weakened, a nuclear option becomes viable—with 'acceptable losses' to us."

The room chilled at the mention of 'acceptable losses.' The officers exchanged glances. Major Wang finally broke the silence. "Do we have a statistical model for these 'acceptable losses'?"

"We do," Li replied. "It's a calculation from our new Algorithm. It's a point of calculated risk. If their defenses fall below a predetermined threshold, we have the go-ahead for full-scale war."

Lieutenant Chu ventured cautiously, "But sir, 'full-scale war' is—"

"That is of course a last resort," Li interrupted. "And that's why we are here—to ensure it doesn't come to that. We continue with cyberattacks to destabilize them enough so they will surrender to our demands, rather than face total war."

"So, it's a balance," mused Major Wang. He oversaw the special branch of The Ministry of State Security (MSS) which controlled its own separate police force for industrial and cyber espionage.

"Yes," said Li.

Wang said, "My MSS agents are in position and will conduct the designated special operations according to your timetable, sir."

"Very well." Li looked pleased. "Captain Zang, prepare the payload. I will personally oversee the launch sequence."

As his team dispersed, Li was left alone with his thoughts and the world's weight on his shoulders.

What does one risk for a future that's secure but may be morally compromised?

An hour later, his team reassembled. "The payload is ready for your command, sir," announced Captain Zhang.

Li looked around the room. These were not just his subordinates. They were patriots, each willing to follow him into the unknown.

Captain Zang said, "This payload is an AI

variant of the *IoT Device Attack*. Its AI helps the virus identify high-value targets and vulnerable systems through reconnaissance and data gathering. It profiles networks and systems to find ones that meet desired criteria for infection. We will use this to strike infrastructure according to the progression plan of Phase III.

Li considered. "Is that the best choice?"

Captain Zang added, "We use this virus to target IoT devices for multiple reasons. For one, most IoT devices don't have enough storage to install proper security measures. These devices often contain easy-to-access data such as passwords and usernames. The virus attaches itself to legitimate files and spreads by infecting other files or programs. We can use them to log into user accounts and steal valuable information, such as more security details."

Li said, "Yes. The *IoT Device Attack* payload could target small devices everywhere, from doorbells to electric generators. But we must also target conventional military devices, from radios to motor ignitions." He paused before adding, "they could lead to military access codes."

He was sure they would cripple critical infrastructure.

"Proceed," he ordered.

As they initiated the attack, General Li felt his weighty responsibility. The game had shifted, and in this high-stakes match, it wasn't about winners—only survivors.

CHAPTER 24

Firewall

Mike sat down at the workstation provided by the National Security Agency. The time was 2:17 a.m., according to the digital clock on the sterile white wall. The room, filled with rows of analysts peering into their monitors, had a subdued urgency. Amber's concerns that more threats were coming proved prescient.

Agent Thompson of the NSA looked at Mike and the Turing team. He didn't bother with formalities. "We've had four more cyberattacks on U.S. infrastructure today. That's why you're here."

Jonah raised an eyebrow. "That bad, huh?"

Despite his calm demeanor, Mike could sense the anxiety gripping the room. Amber's gaze fixated on the West Coast water facilities. Gault looked particularly grave, absorbing the magnitude of the digital assault on the utilities.

Thompson continued, his voice steady but

concerned, "It's not just power. Our rail networks are being tampered with. Signals are getting jammed or misrepresented, leading to halts and, in some cases, collision near misses."

An operator interjected, "There are disruptions in the electrical flow patterns. They're introducing malicious code that's overloading the grid's relay systems."

Tapping her tablet, Amber added, "Water purification plants are also affected. The control systems are being overridden, which could lead to a potential contamination crisis if not addressed."

Gault's brow was furrowed. "What about the commercial sector? Wall Street? Silicon Valley?"

Thompson shook his head. "They've done their homework. This isn't a blind strike. The focus has been on public utilities, aiming to create chaos and panic. Financial institutions are on high alert, but the immediate threat seems directed at basic amenities. And our gasoline distribution isn't spared. Control systems of refineries are being manipulated. While physical reserves remain, the digital controls governing distribution are haywire."

Mike glanced at the screen, his analytical mind racing. "Are they using any specific malware?"

Agent Thompson took a deep breath, "They've deployed a worm we haven't seen before. It's self-propagating and mutates every time we try to isolate it. And it's paired with ransomware that locks critical control systems. However, instead of money, the ransom demands specific access data and security codes."

Mike turned his attention to his monitor. It was blank. He put on his VR glasses and logged into DeepMind. Then, he opened a text editor and started laying down an initial code, calling firewalls, and instructing the system to flag anomalies.

Amber began working on data traffic, creating a filter to alert them to unauthorized access.

Jonah was going deeper, working on identifying the source of the attacks.

The team coordinated through their AI.

Soon, they concentrated on the code and filled the screens with cybersecurity algorithms to create a firewall. The wall was their defense against this cyber assault on the nation's infrastructure.

Amber's eyes widened, "They're not just trying to disrupt; they're extracting information."

Gault looked thoughtful, "It's a two-fold strategy. While we scramble to address the chaos, they access sensitive information, potentially giving them even more power."

After several hours, Thompson's lips tightened into a thin line. "I have more bad news."

Jonah asked, "The disruptions are causing civilian panic?"

"Worse. Multiple military servers have been compromised. We see unfamiliar coding techniques using advanced Name Entity Recognition beyond our expertise. They can pick through our military equipment and pinpoint what gear we have deployed. This allows them to target specific designations and take them out. We need your know-how."

Mike said, "NER is not new, but targeting military gear is. Imagine you're reading a newspaper article. You automatically understand who or what is being talked about, where the events are happening, and other details. NER teaches machines to do the same. It learns to pick out names of people, organizations, locations, and other specifics from a chunk of text."

Thompson nodded.

Mike added, "For example, imagine a picture of Paris at sunset where a woman walks her Dalmatian by the Eiffel Tower. The NER AI can identify "Paris" as a location, "sunset" as a time, "Clara" as a person, "Dalmatian" as a type of dog, and "Eiffel Tower" as a specific location. This information can then be utilized to create a video or artwork that accurately depicts the sentence."

Thompson said, "But an ordinary person wouldn't be privy to military top-secret equipment designations and codes. This hack knows all our stuff."

Amber asked. "What are your priorities?"

"We need to secure the power grids and military databases immediately," Thompson said. "That's your focus."

Hours ticked by. Their eyes were dry, and their backs ached, but the room's tension didn't allow for complaints. The big screen at the front of the room showed an incoming data stream. Mike's code caught several of them as anomalies and shut them down.

Jonah finally said, "I've traced some of the source code. It has markings that tie back to the Chinese military. It is similar to the attacks they used on the Turing Institute."

Mike looked at him. "If we're wrong—"

"We'll wait until we are sure," Amber interjected. "But it's good to know what we're up against."

Mike nodded. "All right. Let's make sure our defenses hold up first. Then we can think about the next move."

The clock blinked at 6:31 a.m. Mike looked at his screen again. For now, they were holding the line. The question was, for how long?

At 9 a.m., Mike was still staring at a monitor. The lines of code scroll by as if they had their own will. It was a mad dance between creation and destruction. For now, he was holding.

"We've got an incoming anomaly—a significant load on the Eastern Seaboard grid," Amber announced, her voice tight but under control.

"Isolate it. I'm deploying countermeasures now." Mike instructed DeepMind to act. His code snaked through the digital labyrinth, seeking out the foreign intruder.

"Done. That attack's been neutralized," Amber confirmed, releasing a subdued sigh of relief.

Jonah glanced at Mike. "Good work, but we're far from being out of the woods."

Just then, Gault walked into the room, a frown marring his usually placid face. "I have to give a status report to the Director of NSA. Do you have anything more?"

"The attack on the civilian infrastructure has been slowed. We've reinforced the firewall protecting military systems. I think we've managed to temporarily contain this virus, Mike said, his eyes meeting Gault's momentarily. But that was enough for Mike to sense something—a cloud of suspicion, maybe even animosity.

"Good," Gault said, nodding curtly before exiting as quickly as he had come in.

Jonah looked at Mike and raised an eyebrow. "He didn't seem too pleased for a man whose ass was being saved."

Mike shrugged, though a nagging thought started to grow in the back of his mind. "Maybe he's just tired. It's been a long night for everyone."

CHAPTER 25

Mole

"Fooling the human in the loop has always been the Achilles' heel in our systems," FBI Agent Miller said, pulling up a holographic screen. An image of a Turing ID pin rotated slowly in the air with every detail magnified. "The heart of the matter is that we trust our eyes and senses. Deep fake technology exploits that."

The overhead lights of the Escher conference room cast long shadows on the whiteboard, where the words "Deep Fake ID" were prominently displayed. The chilling implications of those words hung in the air.

Jonah paced in the Turing workspace, the usual energy in his gait replaced by a ponderous, heavy step. He said, "It's one thing to break through codes and protocols, but to manipulate the system for deceit and infiltration is another level."

Miller showed several holographic articles

showcasing advancements in deep fake technology. "It's astonishing and terrifying in equal measure. Enemy agents are not just creating fake images. They're synthesizing their whole personalities. With the technology at their disposal, they can mirror retina patterns, emulate palm prints, and even mimic DNA sequences."

Gault said, "The notion that a fraud could go through the Turing Institute's corridors unhindered sends a shiver down my spine."

Mike breathed deep and long trying to control his growing sense of concern. The FBI's worry of terrorist using deep fake Turing ID pins meant the entire security program was under scrutiny—something he could ill afford.

Miller asked, "Any ideas how they are doing it?"

Jonah replied, "You'd be surprised. The hacker doesn't need to replicate. They only need to convince. With the right deep fake, they could create a Turing ID pin that appears genuine to every scanner, or human, that sees it. It's possible there is a mole in our inner ranks, and we don't know it."

"The audacity," Amber whispered, her fingers gliding over her tablet as she scanned for vulnerabilities. "They're essentially wielding the Turing brand against itself. They're using our reputation to gain unauthorized access to military facilities."

Mike squirmed in his chair. "But how would they gather the initial data? Our retina scans, palm prints and so on. That's not public information."

Jonah hesitated, his eyes darting to Amber and then Miller. "The hacker could contact a company or service provider pretending to be a specific individual. They would use bits of information—past employment, schools attended, close contacts—and then spin a web of lies to extract further data."

"And that's where deep fake technology shines," Amber added. "They could literally emulate your voice and imitate your mannerisms on a video call. It would appear genuine to an unsuspecting recipient."

The room fell silent.

Miller asked, "So, how do we fight this?"

Gault leaned back, arms folded, eyes thoughtful. "It starts with awareness and education. You must train your staff to double-check and to verify independently. They should be alert to requests that seem out of place or unexpected."

Amber nodded in agreement, "And technically, we might want to consider multi-modal biometrics. Two-factor authentication is good, but in the face of this threat, perhaps three or four factors might be more apt. Our Turing Digital Twin technology is helpful in that."

Jonah said, "We need to strategize our defense against this personal form of attack. One thing was certain, the deep fake threat had only just begun. And it was going to be a battle not just of technology, but of wits, intuition, and the very essence of human trust."

Agent Miller concluded, "And of course, we will need to reexamine every clearance on file."

Mike blanched.

❖ ❖ ❖

The door to Michael Stewart's private rehabilitation room slid open to admit Mike. He was met with the soft strains of Mozart's Symphony No. 40. Michael, clad in a fitted workout ensemble, was undergoing a physical therapy session. He was guided by a holographic avatar that displayed exercises for spinal injury patients. Despite his evident pain, Michael moved with a deliberate grace, each motion carefully calibrated.

In the weeks since his surgery, his recovery exceeded expectations. With the unwavering support of the medical team, he made good progress. His exoskeleton support outfit and AURA's advanced algorithms led to his improvement. The fusion held, his mobility improved, and pain became a diminishing memory. The synergy of man and machine had proven its worth.

Spotting Mike, he paused, motioning for a break. The holograph faded, and Michael gestured towards a comfortable sitting area.

"Mike," he began, a knowing glint in his eyes. "Perfect timing. I've just finished my last set."

Mike sat and asked, "How's the therapy progressing?"

"Every day is a battle," Michael responded, grimacing slightly as he stretched his back, "but one I'm determined to win. Though it seems we're both caught in our own private battle."

Mike nodded, his thoughts swirling. "There's a looming threat against the Algorithm. China's actions are . . . intensifying."

Michael's brow furrowed. "China's intentions have always been clear. But it's not just the Algorithm at stake. It's the control it represents. And you need to ensure that power remains balanced."

Mike sighed, leaning back. "It's not just international politics. Manfred Gault has his suspicions. He's like a bloodhound catching a scent, believing I'm hiding something."

A smirk played on Michael's lips. "Well, he's not wrong, is he?"

Mike's face darkened. "It seems that everybody is probing into every aspect of my life. The FBI is investigating a possible mole or terrorist agents at Turing. And even Amber . . . she's asking questions. Maybe she deserves an answer."

Michael's expression turned stern. "You're talking about revealing our switch, aren't you?"

Mike hesitated before nodding. "She's been through a lot because of me. She deserves to know who she's been with."

"No." Michael's voice was firm. "Telling her would put both of us at risk, and that's not a decision you can make alone. Our identities and our lives are intertwined, Mike. Revealing this secret would endanger me, too."

Their gaze met. The cost of their shared secret was deep. "But it's eating me alive. The lies, the deceit. How do I keep this from her? She's been my anchor through all this."

Michael sighed, running a hand through his hair. "I get it. But we made this decision for a reason, for both our sakes. And it's not fair to burden her with this knowledge, with the weight of this secret."

Silence settled between them. Mike's shoulders slumped in defeat. "It's just . . . every time I look into her eyes, I see that trust, that love. How do I keep lying to her?"

Michael leaned forward. His eyes filled with empathy. "Sometimes, Mike, we must bear the weight of our decisions, no matter how heavy. For now, this secret must remain with us. For everyone's sake."

CHAPTER 26

Truth

Two weeks later, the NSA operations report highlighted a new sinister dimension of cyberattacks: a flood of disinformation. The Chinese were not just attacking infrastructure; they were waging a psychological war.

The Wall Street Journey published:

> . . . social-media platforms are down after an extensive series of cyberattacks. They have been dealing with a flood of misidentified video footage, fabricated information, and violent content. Facebook, X, and TikTok are overwhelmed with false and hateful messages.
>
> The social-media platforms have dedicated large staff and resources to policing false or hateful content, but to no avail. Denial-of-service attacks intermittently

> knocked out consumer websites across the country. The hackers have targeted electrical grids. We have seen phishing attacks multiple ten-fold.
>
> The attempts involved hackers posing as allies and friends who expressed sympathy for them, purporting to offer links to resources that instead contained malware.
>
> You can't really trust anything that is being posted these days.

There were posts falsely alleging that U.S. military bases had been compromised, that naval fleets were in disarray, and that the president was in hiding. Fake videos purported to show riots in major cities, military vehicles patrolling American streets, and citizens being forcibly quarantined in undisclosed locations.

At the Turing Institute, Mike evaluated a series of trending topics from social media platforms. "It's not just about breaking the physical and digital structure. They're trying to break the American spirit."

Amber analyzed the data. "These posts and videos are expertly crafted. Deep fakes, realistic CGI, and voice manipulation. They've mastered the art of creating believable falsehoods."

Jonah, rubbing his temples, muttered, "So, while we're scrambling to combat the cyberattacks, they're instilling panic and distrust among our citizens. The worst part is many are believing what they are seeing. It feeds on itself because some are caught in cognitive dissidence and are unable to escape the false illusions."

Agent Thompson chimed in, "Our assets on the ground report that this misinformation campaign is dual-edged. They're feeding their own populace similar tales. Stories of the U.S. admitting defeat, American soldiers defecting, and U.S. citizens praising the Chinese government for 'freeing' them."

Mike pondered aloud, "It's a classic warfare strategy, reminiscent of the propaganda of World Wars. Break the enemy from within, diminish their morale, while boosting your own."

Gault stood up, pacing the room. "Then we need to counteract it. We have the technology to trace the origins, debunk the fake stories, and expose their lies."

Amber suggested, "We should partner with tech companies and social media platforms. Implement algorithms that can detect these deep fakes in real-time and flag or remove them."

Thompson spoke up, "On the international front, we need to rally our allies. Share intel, expose the misinformation campaign on a global stage. A united front will discredit their lies."

Mike, ever the programmer, was already typing away, "I'm crafting a machine-learning antivirus algorithm. With enough training, it will detect these falsified posts and videos at their source, tagging them for review or removal."

Gault nodded, "Good. But it's not just about removal. People believe what they want to believe. We need to control the narrative, reassure our citizens, and provide them with accurate information."

Amber looked at the team, "We also need to address the mental health consequences. Fear and uncertainty can lead to panic. We need public service announcements, helplines, and community outreach. Counteract the fear with facts and support."

The enormity of the situation was clear. They were not just battling algorithms and servers. They were fighting for the very psyche of their nation.

◆ ◆ ◆

The Turing team's plan was now in motion. Deliberate honest information was fed into the Chinese communications. They hoped it would alter the Chinese Algorithm's predictive models. Mike kept one eye on the monitor and another on the team, each absorbed in the critical task. The room's atmosphere was electric, each minute adding to the tension.

Gault, his eyes never leaving the screen that displayed real-time attack attempts, asked, "Status report?"

Jonah said, "We've successfully rerouted their probes to decoy servers. They're biting."

Amber added, "And our information payload was delivered. They'll miscalculate their next move if their Algorithm takes the bait."

It was a silent waiting game now, a nerve-wracking lull that had everyone on edge.

Mike read the prompt on his screen aloud,

"Incoming communication from NSA. The Chinese are pulling back on some of their more aggressive dispatches."

Gault raised an eyebrow, a glimmer of approval crossing his eyes, "Seems like the bait is working."

But Mike was pensive, "Yes, but why? Their Algorithm is advanced enough to sense a trap. Unless they want us to think we've succeeded."

Frowning while considering the implications, Gault finally spoke, "You think this is a double bluff?"

Mike shrugged, "In a world where AI learns from human behavior and evolves, we can't rule it out. It might be learning to adapt."

Amber looked concerned, "That's a chilling thought. Deceptive algorithms could make cyber warfare unpredictable, turning it into a never-ending game of cat and mouse."

Jonah interjected, "We need to adapt just as fast. The next generation of AI algorithms will likely involve more self-directed machine learning, making them even harder to anticipate."

Gault, standing tall, said, "Then we better make sure we're cats and not mice. We've bought some time. Let's use it wisely."

CHAPTER 27

Enough

Mike settled into his Turing office chair. Its cushion was still molded to the shape of his recent anxiety-ridden fight against hackers. He took a great gulp of coffee and looked at the three monitors displaying various states of the ongoing simulations. One graph was especially troubling—it indicated a spike in cyber activities originating from China.

The sound of a vibrating phone interrupted his troubled thoughts. Gault's terse text message was clear, "Come to my office. Now."

Mike hurriedly saved his work and locked his computer, mentally preparing himself for whatever awaited him. As he navigated the hallways, he couldn't help but anticipate a new crisis.

He knocked on Gault's door and entered. Inside, Gault was not alone. Beside him stood Agent Thompson of the NSA, whose cold, sharp gaze assessing Mike.

Thompson spoke up, his tone crisp and devoid of pleasantries. "Your simulations are edging closer to what we've termed . . . a Pandora's Box."

Gault's hand moved instinctively to straighten a paper on his desk, a simple act revealing his anxiety. "Explain."

Mike interrupted, "My analysis suggests adjustments to the firewall. It's paramount that the entire team is briefed."

Thompson sighed with a hint of exasperation in his eyes. "I don't think we can afford the luxury of team consensus."

Not one to back down, Mike responded, "Blind haste could prove costlier."

After a tense pause, Gault said, "I have to agree."

He called an emergency briefing.

Soon, the cream of the Turing team assembled in the Escher conference room with its advanced technology displays.

Mike launched into his presentation. The screen flashed graphs of covert operations and infographics. There were hacking signatures sprawled on the display. He dove into the clandestine world of cyber espionage. He asked Thompson to lay bare the contrasting strategies of the world's superpowers.

Thompson said, "In cyberspace, borders dissolve, and nations engage in a constant silent war. It is a complex web of espionage, deception, and strategy. It is led by the USA, China, and Russia."

Amber and Jonah sat up front and looked

intently at the screen.

Thompson continued. "The National Security Agency (NSA) and Cyber Command (USCYBERCOM) lead the charge on defense and offensive, respectively. The NSA programs focus on safeguarding critical infrastructure. It combats cyberterrorism and protects national secrets."

The audience was intrigued, watching closely.

Mike took over. "China's cyber approach is best described as stealthy and opportunistic. Their operations are notorious for their well-orchestrated disinformation campaigns. In comparison, Russia's expertise lies in its disinformation warfare. They have mastered creating chaos. They influence political narratives and destabilize adversaries without firing a bullet. Their tactics are not just about hacking systems but hacking minds."

He paused.

"Economically, Russia does not have a comparable technology. This often limits the scale of its operations. International sanctions have isolated Russia digitally. This has led to a technological gap. However, this week, the President of Russia is in Beijing to lend his support to its signature Belt and Road Initiative, which for past decades has used railroads, ports, and other projects to expand Chinese economic influence abroad. We are skeptical of the Chinese initiative's intentions."

Gault said, getting straight to the point. "We're facing an unprecedented crisis. We've learned that Russia may be supporting China's cyberattacks. We don't know how far they are willing to go. But everything is now even more complicated. The Algorithm that China has developed by stealing our technology helps develop the cyberattacks. This could bring us to the brink of a war."

He paused, letting the weight of his words sink in. Jonah spoke out, "So, we're talking about a game theory strategy from the enemy Algorithm?"

"Exactly," Mike confirmed. "But that's not all. There are indications of an unknown variable within the Algorithm that we don't fully comprehend."

The room was thick with concern about the potential problem they were grappling with.

Amber broke the silence. "What can we do?"

"That's why I'm here. To ask you that question," said Thompson.

There was a long silence that seemed to stretch beyond endurance.

Then Mike said, "We need to make a significant revision to our Algorithm. It must become our primary antivirus cybersecurity. The new version should withstand the escalating attacks and be flexible enough to adapt."

Gault chimed in from the back of the room. "That would give the Algorithm a measure of autonomy that we have tried to avoid."

Mike said, "I agree. It's a fine line between protecting us from outsiders to protecting us from the Algorithm itself."

The words hung ominously throughout the room.

"Do you have a plan for this highly ambitious endeavor?" asked Gault.

Mike gazed at Gault, sensing his skepticism. I propose we develop real-time human-in-the-loop Deep Reenforcement Learning. It will train the next Algorithm iteration. This will allow us to incorporate our newly learned insights. It will stop hackers and adapt quickly."

Gault raised an eyebrow. "Real-time Human-supervised? Are you suggesting we continuously update and instruct the Algorithm on specific anti-hacking tools?"

"Given the stakes, yes, I am."

"The last thing we need is an autonomous Algorithm making decisions that could lead to a military confrontation," insisted Gault.

The room was still for a moment, each member of the Turing team wrestling with the problem.

Thompson interjected, "I don't think we have an alternative. Do we?"

Finally, Gault nodded. "Alright, we can work toward that goal, but no changes will be made without full review and evaluation by our engineering team of Dr. Helen Martinez and Dr. Chetna Wu."

Mike frowned. "Time is not on our side."

Gault said, "Full review and evaluation!"

As the team dispersed to their respective stations, Mike felt the world's weight on his shoulders. But he sensed a collective resolve in the room for the first time. They were a united front in the face of an

impending disaster. But he still had to create the code that would achieve his goals.
Will it be enough?

CHAPTER 28

Dangling Over the Edge

Amber, Mike, and Jonah teetered over the edge of the high building terrace, legs dangling into the void as the city's underbelly pulsed below them. Amber's hair quivered under the caress of the clandestine wind. City lights blinked like dying stars, vying for attention in the evening haze.

Breaking through the hush, Mike offered, "It's peculiar how shifting your vantage point can obliterate the problems you thought were insurmountable."

Jonah glanced sideways, his eyebrows knitting together.

"Are we back to AI existentialism?" Amber prodded, her head tipping just so.

"Touché!" A grin flickered across Mike's face. "I am recalling Einstein from our university days."

Jonah smirked. "Ah, yes. The puzzle of spacetime—on a rooftop. Classic you."

Mike said, "Einstein reconciled Newtonian mechanics and Maxwell's equations by swapping out the constancy of time for the constancy of light. His brilliant trick was to displace one's focus to see things anew. Much like the difficulties we are encountering with the Chinese Algorithm."

Amber's eyes grew somber. "A compelling analogy. Reframe the problem."

"Exactly. Our gaze needs readjusting," Jonah contributed, rubbing his chin in a bemused fashion.

Mike lifted his drink. "Like our continual tweaking of the Algorithm. What if we're not up against a mounting war of innumerable cyberattacks but a limited perspective?"

Amber leaned closer. Her interest piqued. "You're suggesting that the enemy's intentions are not limited to cyberattacks?"

Mike shrugged. "We're too enmeshed in the minutiae to see the Chinese Algorithm for what it is. We are thinking of it as a benign servant, like our Algorithm."

Amber exhaled deeply. "So how do we adjust our view? How do we discern the Chinese Algorithm anew?"

Jonah's eyes narrowed, a glint of realization dawning. "Yes, maybe our fundamental understanding is misaligned. How do you see the Chinese Algorithm?"

"As an indifferent autonomous War Gamer!" said Mike.

A colder and more insistent wind surged

around them, whispering veiled menaces. It seemed like something nefarious was beckoning them into a deeper game.

Mike's forehead tightened. "What if these cyberattacks and paradox anomalies are smokescreens masking a deeper intrusion?"

Amber's eyes widened. "That would signify an orchestrated campaign beyond crippling our national grid. These attacks might be just red herrings. What do you think their real intentions are?"

Mike's jaw set firm. "A cyber offensive on conventional military target so demanding that it may cloak a deeper cyber threat to our nuclear deterrence."

Amber said, "That would be an act of war."

Jonah's voice grew thick. "But who stands to gain from destabilizing us?"

Amber's fingers trembled. "China could be inundating our system with cyberattacks, ensnaring us in a computational quagmire. Then they could make a move, leveraging their nuclear arsenal."

Jonah clenched his fists. "A subversive strategy to blindside us, keeping us preoccupied with data decoy attacks."

Mike's eyes smoldered. "So, in grappling with these paradox anomalies, we're just pawns in their larger scheme?"

Amber nodded gravely. "We need to trace this malignancy to its root and sever it before it metastasizes further."

Mike said, "We may have kept them off so far,

but I can't shake the feeling that they're adapting faster. Their Algorithm is like an evolving predator. We're playing by someone else's rules. It's time to make our own."

Amber nodded, sharing his concern. "So, what do we do? The NSA is already stretched thin. Our virtual firewall is about as robust as it's going to get."

Gazing upwards, he added, "To stop the Chinese Algorithm, we must manipulate it. We change tactics." Mike's eyes narrowed. "Instead of just defending, we figure out a way to disable the Chinese Algorithm, or at least impede its learning and adapting capabilities."

Jonah said, "We can barely understand our own Algorithm. We are constantly concerned with making changes that can lead to unwanted consequences."

Amber considered this momentarily, and then her eyes brightened. "What if we introduced an element it couldn't predict? Something so illogical and human that it would send their Algorithm into a loop, trying to understand it? Can we do that?"

Mike sighed. "I don't know yet, but we must think of something soon. If we're playing a game of illusions with an AI, we'll eventually lose."

He gazed into her eyes and added, "It can think faster and adapt quicker."

CHAPTER 29

Diabolus Ex Machina

General Li sat rigid in his chair, staring at the encrypted message flashing on his computer screen. The corners of his lips tightened. The report said, "China's cyberspace approach reflects an ambitious, centralized, and relentless national strategy."

He turned his gaze to the three officers standing before him. They led his elite Unit 398. It had a reputation for advanced persistent threats to infiltrate foreign networks. It had been repeatedly singled out by the West. A fact they took pride in.

"High command has issued new orders," General Li began, locking eyes with each subordinate. "We are transitioning from cyber chaos measures to Phase IV. I want your thoughts."

Captain Zhang's worry was printed on his face. He said, "Our new AI system will learn to mutate and change the code of the virus to avoid signature-based anti-virus detection. It could also learn which behaviors and payloads are more likely to avoid triggering heuristic and behavioral detection systems. However, Phase IV includes direct attacks on America's nuclear deterrent air, sea, and land facilities, sir."

Li stood stone-faced.

Zhang muttered quietly, "Their response could be . . . significant."

He cast his eyes down.

Li turned to the screen displaying the intrusion vectors, concealed through layers of proxy servers. "We've been meticulous in our defense. But even if they do respond, we will have achieved the 'probabilistic advantage'."

Zhang looked properly chastened.

Major Wang said, "I've already installed my agents. They've been briefed. I have absolute faith they will execute their mission flawlessly, sir."

Li nodded.

Lieutenant Chu said, "Our surveillance systems are in place to monitor the response, sir."

Li said, "Prepare the package."

Several hours later, they reconvened.

"Sir," Captain Zhang said hesitantly. "The Phase IV package is ready."

Li said, "Release the *Serpent*."

CHAPTER 30

Dev Con II

In the late hours of the evening, Mike found himself immersed in his dimly lit workspace. His attention shifted from screens filled with complex algorithms to the scattered academic papers on Deep Reenforcement Learning that covered his desk. A cup of once-steaming coffee had grown cold, abandoned amidst his pursuit of a disturbing puzzle.

The source of his unease lay in a recent exploration of Human-in-the-Loop AI Learning—a concept where the Algorithm learned under human guidance. Originally conceived as a safety mechanism, a check to prevent AI from spiraling out of control, it had served as a moral compass. But his deep dive into Chinese Algorithm data had unearthed unsettling anomalies.

Amber's entrance into the room disrupted his contemplation. Her eyes, though fatigued, held a keen alertness as she settled into the chair beside him.

"Late night?" she inquired.

Mike cautiously began, "Yes, and I've stumbled upon a significant issue. The Chinese Algorithm's behavior doesn't align with the typical characteristics of Human-supervised training."

Amber leaned close; her interest piqued. "Please, explain."

Mike continued, "It's possible they're utilizing unsupervised liquid neural networks. We've explored similar networks for training our Algorithm, drawing inspiration from the dynamic connections between brain cells. In the human brain, synapses are in constant flux, enabling adaptation to new information and changing environments."

Amber considered his words, her expression thoughtful. "So, you're suggesting that their next-gen AI algorithms might be on the brink of autonomously directing their own machine learning—a system evolving its ruthlessness exponentially."

Mike pressed on, his concerns mounting. "Precisely. And what if this design allows the Algorithm to calculate 'acceptable losses' in human lives while pursuing its strategic objectives? What criteria would it use?"

Amber's eyes widened as she grasped the implications. "You're suggesting a system where the Algorithm not only strives to win but also determines a 'human cost' it deems 'acceptable.'

Amber took a moment to absorb the gravity of Mike's findings. "That's beyond terrifying; it fundamentally alters our understanding of the threat we face."

Their discussion was abruptly interrupted by the intrusion of NSA Director Steve Altman, accompanied by his retinue. They marched into the center of the workstation gallery.

"Circle up," Altman commanded, dispelling any formalities. He threw a large folder on the desk in front of him. It was marked:

TOP SECRET

EYES ONLY

It had additional clandestine operational words stamped in every corner.

The assembled computer scientists formed a tight circle around the visiting officials, an aura of urgency permeating the room.

Altman delivered disquieting news. "Two hours ago, we detected a cyber intrusion into one of our most secure databases. It contained top-secret launch codes for our nuclear arsenal."

A chilling silence descended upon the room.

Altman continued, explaining the robust design of the U.S. nuclear triad—missiles, bombers, and submarines—designed to be impervious to digital threats.

He said, "This recent breach has raised alarming questions. The President elevated the nation's defense posture to DEV CON II. He signed an executive order authorizing rapid advances in cybersecurity artificial intelligence for the national security arsenal."

Mike's stomach tightened with apprehension, and Director Altman posed a daunting challenge to the Turing team: "Can your team uncover how we became vulnerable to these latest cyber strategies?"

"What's the extent of the breach?" Gault asked, his voice betraying no emotion.

"We're still assessing. But our internal alarms flagged it as originating from a Chinese IP address," Director Altman continued. "We've managed to limit the breach for now, but this indicates a coordinated plan. Possibly preparation for a nuclear first strike."

Jonah interjected; his voice tinged with disbelief. "Are you suggesting that the enemy could effectively blind our systems and then launch an attack without immediate retaliation?"

Altman responded with a solemn nod. "That's correct."

A complex interplay of logic and dread flickered across Amber's face as her eyes met Mike's.

Gault leaned forward, his gaze narrowing. "How can our Turing team assist in this critical situation?"

Altman wasted no time. "Your expertise is crucial in tracing the malware's origins and devising a strategy to counteract its actions. Time is of the essence."

Mike felt his hands clenching into fists.

Gault continued probing. "So, you believe that your command systems can't keep up with the evolving threats?"

Altman replied resolutely, "Exactly. However,

it's important to remember that each segment of the triad operates with its dedicated, isolated circuitry and command protocols."

Amber shifted in her chair, her eyes narrowing. "But isolation can be a double-edged sword. What if the enemy infiltrates a specific unit? Without real-time updates, that unit could remain isolated and vulnerable."

Altman interjected, "Our nuclear command and control systems are designed to be isolated from the standard military network, making them resistant to traditional cyberattacks. However, resistant doesn't equate to invulnerable. Human checks and constant internal auditing play a crucial role in maintaining their integrity. The NSA routinely conducts counter-infiltration operations to safeguard these units."

Mike, running his fingers through his hair. "While that provides some comfort, we should also consider the possibility of a hybrid attack—cyber infiltration followed by physical sabotage. If they manage to compromise even one critical person within the system..."

Gault interrupted, completing Mike's thought. "We'd be facing a catastrophic failure. What's the countermeasure?"

Without hesitation, Mike responded, "Strengthening internal defenses is imperative. Think of it as building a castle with multiple walls. If an adversary breaches the outer wall, they should face yet another, and another."

Director Altman concurred. "Layers of security,

redundant systems, and vigilant human oversight are our best defense. We have credible evidence that this cyberattack originated from Chinese servers. Given the escalating tensions and the intelligence we've gathered, we believe this is a probing attack—a test of our defenses before a potential strike."

Amber inquired, "Do you have any specific information about the cyber-attack package?"

Altman revealed, "Yes. It's all in these documents I'm leaving with you."

He pointed to the folder he had thrown on the desk.

He added, "We've identified the attack as a completely new type of malware. It has an AI system that tests and iterates to determine the most damaging payloads while avoiding detection. It is completely self-directed by its own AI payload which is smarter and more adaptable than anything you can imagine. It boldly named itself *Serpent*. "

Mike turned to Director Altman and asked, "What's the current assessed readiness of the U.S. nuclear deterrence?"

Altman replied with concern, "That's classified of course, but normally, we maintain a 94.5% state of readiness due to maintenance and repair of various elements. However, the status is in flux. I'm heading back to my command center. Please keep me informed of your progress. I'm relying on your expertise."

With a sense of gratitude in his eyes, Altman said, "The NSA values collaboration with your team. We're navigating uncharted waters, but together, we can weather this storm."

As Altman and his entourage departed, a few experts remained to collaborate with the Turing team.

Gault wasted no time taking charge of the situation. "Alright, we'll initiate a comprehensive review to identify vulnerabilities. We'll work closely with the NSA and Cyber Command to fortify our existing systems. Meanwhile, Stewart, your task is to fine-tune the Algorithm and monitor for any anomalies within our nuclear command and control."

"Consider it done," Mike affirmed.

Amber added, "This changes everything, doesn't it?"

Mike met her gaze with a determined nod. "Yes, it's a game-changer. Until now, they have only targeted civilian and conventional military infrastructure. They meticulously avoided our nuclear deterrence. Now, the real question is, how do you counter a Chinese Algorithm that's constantly learning and evolving its methods of destruction? The machine learning models we've known were based on some level of ethical responsibility. This Chinese Algorithm knows no bounds."

Gault chimed in, "I'll reach out to our contacts in the Pentagon. If this escalates further, we might need more than just digital countermeasures."

Amber glanced at Mike.

He said, "We're on it. I'll start by isolating the potentially compromised NSA networks. Then, I'll work on developing a digital antidote for the *Serpent*."

CHAPTER 31

War Games

Mike settled back into his chair. His screen filled with lines of code, each line representing a defense against the impending cyber onslaught.

Hours passed like minutes as the team worked seamlessly through the early hours of the morning. Many of the workstations around the gallery were still occupied with dedicated scientists.

Eventually, Mike went to Amber.

"Hey, are you alright?" he asked.

Amber looked up, snapping back to the present. "Yeah, I'm fine. Just processing, you know?"

Mike understood. "It's tough to catch a break these days. Here, I brought you some coffee."

"Thanks."

He handed her a cup.

Gault approached them and asked, "I want to hear your opinion. Can our Algorithm predict a nuclear strike?" He shifted his gaze towards Mike.

Mike responded thoughtfully, aware of the enormity of the challenge. "Our Algorithm is designed to adapt and counter various cyber threats. But predicting a nuclear strike under these conditions involves more variables than we've trained it for."

Gault's concern was evident in his voice as he asked, "What are our options?"

Clearing his throat, Mike explained cautiously. "We could expedite the implementation of a specialized module into the Algorithm. It would conduct simulations to predict outcomes based on real-time data. However, I must emphasize that the outcome is uncertain at best."

Gault said, "I am authorizing you to proceed."

Mike nodded firmly. "I'll get started immediately, but I'll require Amber's expertise."

Gault turned to Amber, giving her a direct order. "Make it happen."

❖ ❖ ❖

The next day, the hum of servers filled the dimly lit Turing team office as Mike and Amber worked diligently. Their dual monitors displayed intricate webs of code and simulated outcomes; evidence of hours spent on the war games module.

Amber brought up a technical suggestion. "Can we introduce a parameter here to consider human decision-making variables?"

She pointed at a complex line of code.

Mike evaluated the proposal. "Incorporating that parameter could enhance the depth of our predictions. It's a good idea."

Just as Amber was about to respond, Gault entered the room, his eyes scanning the lines of code on the monitors before settling on Mike.

Gault inquired with a hint of suspicion in his tone, "How's the module coming along?"

Mike, cautious of Gault's growing skepticism, replied carefully, "We're on the verge of running the initial test simulation."

Gault issued a stern warning. "It had better yield useful results, or our jobs—and potentially more —will be on the line."

He left the room as abruptly.

Amber, concerned about the situation, sighed, and rubbed her temples. "He seems odd."

Mike shared his unease. "I think he's been delving into my background. He's become increasingly suspicious of me lately."

Amber shook her head and said, "Things are already complicated enough."

"I'll tread carefully," Mike concluded.

An hour later, as they ran the first test of the war game module, the room fell into silence. Data streams filled the screens with probability matrices, potential outcomes, and escalation scenarios—a mesmerizing yet horrifying sight.

The terminal blinked with the words:

"SIMULATION COMPLETE!"

Mike, with a sense of anticipation, pressed a key to reveal the results. A graph materialized, showing a disturbingly high likelihood of nuclear escalation if certain cyber-attack patterns persisted.

Amber's response was measured. "That's... not good."

Mike furrowed his brow, contemplating the gravity of the situation. "This raises a haunting question: What constitutes 'acceptable losses'?"

"If the Chinese have a specific threshold in mind, a point at which they believe victory is assured," Mike continued, "we must determine what that threshold is. Is it when they compromise our defense networks? Is it when they incapacitate a certain number of our military assets? What's their equivalent *Spitfire Rule*?"

Jonah asked, "What's a *Spitfire Rule*?"

Mike explained, "The *Spitfire Rule* is a tipping point. During World War II, the British had a certain number of Spitfire fighters. The Germans based their decision to invade England on the number of remaining British fighters. The Germans chose the number 600—if the British fighter strength fell below that, the Germans would invade. The British never disclosed their actual strength, but it hovered close to 600 for a considerable period."

Jonah nodded with understanding.

Mike continued, "So, I've designated the nuclear deterrence tipping point as the *Spitfire Rule*. The challenge is that we don't know what the Chinese

Algorithm has set as its tipping point."

The room seemed to contract with the weight of their concerns.

Gault, sitting with his arms crossed, said, "So, what can we do about it?"

Mike gestured towards a large display at the front of the conference room. "This is the culmination of our efforts—code-crunching and data analysis. These war games simulate not only cyberattacks but also the geopolitical implications and decision-making processes."

As Mike toggled a few keys, the screen illuminated the results of real-time simulation models.

Jonah inquired, "Could you explain the decision-making processes?"

Mike elaborated, "We've integrated game theory algorithms to simulate various countries, providing responses to diverse scenarios, including both rational and irrational decision-making. Crucially, we've included 'acceptable losses' as a parameter."

A palpable silence hung in the room.

Gault finally broke the silence. "Acceptable losses? That sounds like a risky calculation."

Mike acknowledged the unsettling nature of the concept. "It is unsettling, but it's likely a component of the Chinese strategy. If they have their version of the *Spitfire Rule*, a threshold where they believe the odds tilt in their favor, they may resort to even more drastic actions, including a nuclear attack."

Gault studied Mike, his gaze penetrating. "And

how do you propose we determine this threshold?"

Mike glanced at Amber, and with her nod, he continued. "By conducting a series of advanced simulations, incorporating real-world data and assumptions, we can attempt to reverse-engineer their strategy. But to do so effectively, we'll need access to classified intelligence on the Chinese Algorithm."

Gault, intrigued but cautious, questioned further. "And do you believe you can secure us that access?"

Mike paused, carefully choosing his words. "I believe it's worth trying. The stakes couldn't be higher."

Gault, seemingly out of patience, concluded, "Run your simulations. If this turns out to be a wild goose chase, it's on you."

As the meeting dispersed, Mike looked up and caught Amber's eye. She looked worried. He felt a knot tighten in his stomach but pushed it aside. Right now, he had to focus on the problem at hand—calculating the incalculable, understanding the mindset of a machine who saw the world as nothing more than numbers on a balance sheet. Even if those numbers included human lives."

Mike said, "We have to ask the Algorithm to calculate the *Spitfire Rule* for this circumstance."

Amber said, "How would our Algorithm do that?"

Mike said, "I have no idea, but I'll bet we get an answer."

Amid this tension, the Algorithm quietly computed the *Spitfire Rule*, its algorithms whirring in the background. It analyzed vast datasets, historical precedents, and real-time intelligence. All the while running machine learning models to predict the unpredictable. As it arrived at the unsettling percentage, the room seemed to chill.

It reported the war threshold for the US nuclear state of readiness in bold red letters:

11.723%.

The Algorithm reported, "At this percentage of US nuclear deterrence readiness, it would be advantageous for China to attack. Their elite would survive in an underground shelter while they could launch an all-out nuclear war with over one thousand thermal nuclear missiles. They could expect less than 100 U.S. responding missiles."

The conclusion hung in the air, a stark reminder of the precarious situation they were in. It was as if the machine had glimpsed into the abyss. Now the team had to grapple with the alarming truth. They were standing at the edge of the unknown, facing an adversary that operated without bounds, all while their creation calculated the unthinkable.

Could we endure that?
What is our state of readiness?

CHAPTER 32

Night Out

The night was clear, and the city buzzed with life as Mike and Michael stepped out of a sleek black car in front of a luxurious restaurant. It was a rare treat for Mike to escape the confines of the Turing Institute and enjoy a night on the town. The valet took their car with a nod, and they entered the restaurant, greeted by the soft glow of chandeliers and the murmur of conversation.

"Quite a place you've picked, Michael," Mike remarked, glancing around at the opulent décor.

Michael grinned, his eyes reflecting the excitement of the evening. "Only the best for a night like this, my friend. Besides, we deserve a break after weeks the chaos."

They were led to a private table with a view of the city skyline. The aroma of exquisite cuisine filled the air, and they eagerly perused the menu. As they sipped on fine wine and savored each meticulously crafted dish, they delved into conversation.

"You know, Mike," Michael began, "this AI spinal fusion surgery has been a game-changer for me. I couldn't have imagined a few years ago that I'd celebrate here and enjoy this incredible meal."

Mike nodded. His eyes were filled with genuine happiness for his friend. "It's amazing how far AI has come in healthcare. The physical therapy and rehabilitation programs tailored to your needs have been a revelation."

Michael's gaze turned contemplative. "I've been thinking a lot about my future, Mike. Soon, I will be able to live a normal life. Thanks to you and AI, I have a second chance. I want to make the most of it."

Mike knew where this was leading, and he felt a pang of guilt. "Michael, there's something I need to tell you."

Their conversation turned to the ongoing investigations at the Turing Institute. Mike voiced his concerns. "I can't shake the feeling that Gault's investigation is becoming more intrusive."

Mike sighed. His brow furrowed. "I know, and there's also talk of a possible mole hunt by the FBI on the Turing grounds. The tension is ratcheting up."

Michael gazed into the distance. "It's a dangerous game we're playing, Mike. We need to be cautious and watch our every step."

Their expressions grew somber as they discussed the looming threat from China and the Algorithm.

"I feel concern," Michael admitted, his voice

tinged with vulnerability. "Fear, anger, but also a strange sense of determination. We can't let the Chinese Algorithm and its potential for destruction go unchecked."

Mike leaned close. " We've been dealing with the *Serpent* attack for two weeks. It's relentless. We can't underestimate the Chinese Algorithm. Its capacity to learn and adapt is beyond anything we've seen before. It's like a relentless force that keeps evolving, and we cannot predict its next move."

Michael's eyes shone with determination. "But we can't lose hope. You've made incredible strides in countering cyber threats. Our Algorithm has the potential to be a powerful tool in this battle."

Mike smiled, appreciating Michael's optimism. "You're right. Our Algorithm is a beacon of hope, a creation that can help us safeguard our digital and physical world."

Michael held up a hand, stopping him. "Enough. No more tonight, Mike. This is our night to relax and enjoy. We'll deal with everything else later."

Mike nodded, though the weight of his secrets gnawed at him.

"I need to tell Amber about us," said Mike.

"We've already discussed this before. It's unfair. Unfair to me and unfair to her. After all, we've just been discussing investigations by the FBI, Gault, and moles. You think this is possible."

"Shut up and let me think!" said Mike.

"That's right, think. You need to get a grip."

"We need to muddy the waters as much as

possible so no one can get traction on our ID."

"That's on you."

Mike said, "Okay. Okay, you're right. But sooner or later, it will happen."

"Perhaps. But not yet."

CHAPTER 33

Return Fire

"They're not just targeting our IT systems," Mike declared. "Satellite links, communication Systems, even missile launch codes, are under assault. Nothing is safe. I don't think we can last another week under this bombardment."

"Amber, analyzing a portion of the compromised code, looked up, "They're upgrading their AI-enhanced *Serpent.* It's adapting. Every time we put up a defense, it learns, evolves, and finds a way around."

Mike said, "Look here." He pointed at a map highlighting the affected areas. "They're focusing on Norfolk Naval Base, Fort Bragg, and Joint Base Andrews. It's causing a systematic breakdown of command-and-control systems."

Gault's face turned grim. "That's not all. They've also infiltrated the West Coast defense systems—

Naval Base San Diego, Camp Pendleton. Our fleet readiness is compromised as we speak."

Amber froze. "The Pacific Fleet . . . if they manage to immobilize it, we'll have significant exposure. They could be preparing for a physical assault, maybe in Taiwan."

Mike thought of the broader implications. "And with our communication lines disrupted, coordinating a defense, or even maintaining our forward bases becomes a challenge. Our overseas troops will be isolated."

Gault added, "We've had two drones go off-course over hostile territories. That risks international incidents. Our missile defense systems are glitchy. If this continues, our military readiness and deterrence capabilities will be severely undermined. I hesitate to think what per centage it has already fallen from the initial level."

As they delved deeper into the attack's intricacies, a realization dawned. The Chinese weren't just crippling the US defense. They were sending a clear message to allies and adversaries alike about the vulnerabilities of the American military.

"We need a multi-pronged approach," Mike stated, determination in his eyes. "First, we fortify and restore our communication lines. We need to ensure ground troops, naval fleets, and air squadrons can coordinate. Secondly, we track the source of these attacks—not just the digital origin, but the physical location. If they're using an AI-enhanced worm, they must have a substantial server facility supporting it."

Amber looked at Mike, understanding the dawn. "I think we should consider a physical counter-operation."

Mike nodded. "If we can exactly locate the hub of their operations, a strategic military strike could cripple them."

Gault, rubbing his temples, sighed, "This is uncharted territory. But we're out of options. Stewart, work on locating that facility. Amber, see if you can devise malware to feed them the wrong intel. If we can make them blind, even momentarily, it'll give us an advantage. I'll update the NSA and offer our suggestion of a military strike. They will need time to get military assets in position."

The challenges were mounting, and the stakes had never been higher. As the trio got to work, they knew that the battles being fought in the digital realm would have profound real-world consequences.

Mike leaned back in his chair, pushing back his hair, considering the possibility of a retaliatory decision.

◆ ◆ ◆

The NSA responded to Turing's strike suggestion by making air force assets ready in Guam. As a last resort they would eliminate the Chinese cyberattack command.

Agent Thompson came to Turing and said, "Our estimated readiness for nuclear strategic deterrence has fallen to 37.3%. We can't let this continue.

The State Department has received a communication from China with demands. They want the US to immediately cease all military activities in the western Pacific, including Japan, the Philippines, Guam, and Midway. They demand that all ships, planes, and military ground forces withdraw in four weeks."

Everyone was in shock.

"We can retaliate," Mike began, looking at Thompson. "If the Algorithm can trace back the exact origin of the *Serpent*. We could then counter-attack their cyberinfrastructure."

Thompson frowned, his experience with international conflicts evident. "Launching a military strike as part of a cyber counter-offensive would probably escalate the situation into a full-blown conventional war."

Gault looked contemplative. "As much as I'd like to fight back, you're right. We should prioritize defense and neutralize the threat. He paused, looking at Mike. "But we should be prepared with a countermeasure as an option for our leadership."

Mike nodded. "Understood. While I work on the antidote for the *Serpent*, Amber can create a 'shadow worm.' Something we can deploy that'll not only trace back to its origin but also lie dormant in their system. If we're pushed into a corner, it can reveal their operations location."

Agent Thompson raised an eyebrow. "A digital sleeper agent?"

Mike said, "Exactly. It's discreet and won't

directly harm their infrastructure unless activated."

Amber looked thoughtful. "A 'shadow worm' can also gather intelligence. It could help us better understand their next moves."

Gault turned to Thompson and asked, "What's the government's stance on this? Will there be repercussions if we proceed with cyber retaliation and hold off on a military strike?"

Thompson asked, "Right, but what if the other side, the Chinese Algorithm, uses a different approach? Do you think the Chinese Algorithm calculates 'acceptable losses' as a specific probability?"

Mike said, "Yes. And if our nuclear deterrence defenses reach a specific weak point, the Chinese Algorithm may decide to go all in and risk a nuclear strike."

◆ ◆ ◆

It was only hours later that NSA agent Thompson reported, "The situation is fluid. Our nuclear operation readiness has fallen to 30%. The President and the National Security Council are in continuous sessions. Your military strike countermeasure might be the card we need to play very soon."

Mike took a deep breath, "The Algorithm can cross-check multiple data points and verify the exact source location of the cyberattack."

Amber added, "While preparing our digital arsenal, we should bolster our defenses. If they've used the *Serpent* this time, there's no telling what else they have up their sleeves."

Thompson said, "We can't just be on the defensive. We need to strike back to halt their progress and show them we won't be pushed around."

An agent from the CIA agreed. "Our assets on the ground in China have relayed some prime targets. Dams, power grids, and transportation networks. We can cripple them."

Amber interjected, "I've identified vulnerabilities in their communication infrastructure. With a multi-vector assault, we can disrupt their cyber command and control nodes."

Mike nodded, focusing on his screen. "I can design a cyber worm, a sibling of their own AI-enhanced malware. It will not only disrupt their operations but also feed them disinformation. They'll be fighting ghosts."

Thompson, with a sharp edge to his voice, said, "While the digital front keeps them busy, our CIA operatives in Beijing and Shanghai will gather intel on their next moves and sabotage their digital hubs."

Gault, always the strategist, pondered, "This is initiating a two-front war. One digital, the other physical. It's risky. The international community might not see this as a defensive action."

Mike responded, "It's a necessary risk. The digital strike is a diversion. The real work will be done on the ground by the CIA. We're just creating an environment for them to operate."

Amber added, "This isn't just about retaliation.

It's about restoring balance. Showing them that every action has consequences."

CHAPTER 34

Hammer

Andrews Air Force Base sprawled across the landscape, a formidable testament to military might. The tarmac glistened beneath the scorching sun, a vast expanse of concrete, interrupted only by sleek, powerful aircraft parked in precise formation. The air carried the metallic tang of jet fuel. The hum of engines and the distant roar of jet planes provided a constant auditory backdrop to the visual spectacle.

Mike, Amber, and Jonah stood in the heart of the base, surrounded by the sounds of military aircraft and active military operations. They had received an urgent call from Agent Thompson, requesting their presence at the Air Force command center.

As they entered the center, they were met with a flurry of activity. Military personnel were huddled around screens displaying maps and data feeds. On one wall, a large digital map of Asia showed China's vast expanse, and a blinking red marker indicated the target: Unit 398.

General Ramirez, the commanding officer of the base, approached them.

"Thank you for coming on such short notice," he said, his tone a mixture of urgency and determination. "We've been monitoring Unit 398's activities as you suggested. Their cyberattacks are causing significant damage to our infrastructure and military capabilities."

Amber nodded. "We understand the situation. What's your plan?"

Ramirez motioned for them to follow him to a secure briefing room. Inside, they found a team of military analysts gathered around a large conference table. The room was equipped with state-of-the-art communication systems.

Ramirez said, " Unit 398 has set up a well-protected base in a remote region of China. Our mission is to cripple their capabilities."

Mike leaned forward. "How will you do that?"

"We were hoping to get specific direction from your team to do that."

The general activated a holographic projection of the target area. It showed a sprawling complex nestled deep within the Chinese mainland.

Mike said, "Our intelligence indicates that Unit 398's operations center is located here," he said, pointing to a large facility. "They've also established a server farm."

The general studied the hologram. "And the

electric grid?"

Amber continued, "The electric grid supplying power to their base is vulnerable. We believe that by disabling it, you can disrupt their operations significantly."

Jonah interjected, pointing to additional buildings, "What about their main computer center? If we take that out, it should cripple their ability to coordinate cyberattacks."

General Ramirez nodded in agreement. "Exactly. Our mission is to coordinate an airstrike that targets these key elements that you've identified. We'll use small but highly accurate munitions."

Mike raised an important question, "How do we ensure that we hit these targets precisely?"

The general turned to his team, and a military analyst stepped forward. "We have flight crews located in Guam, flying B-2 Spirit stealth bombers. These aircraft are equipped with advanced targeting systems and precision-guided munitions. The hypersonic cruise missiles will penetrate Chinese air defense and take out the targets. We have real-time communication with the flight crews, and they'll receive the updated coordinates you've provided."

Amber chimed in, "What's the timeframe for the mission?"

General Ramirez glanced at his watch. "The bombers will be in the air and en route to the target when USCYBERCOM reports that we have reached the critical point you've designated. Then we will act quickly to execute the mission."

Mike nodded. "Let's speak with the flight crew and provide them with the latest coordinates. We can assist in the real-time adjustments using our technology."

The team immediately got to work. Amber and Jonah established a secure communication link with the flight crew, relaying the coordinates and ensuring they had the most up-to-date information. Mike monitored the preparation of the operation from the command center, ready to provide technical assistance if needed.

As the minutes passed, tension filled the room. The fate of the mission hung in the balance, and the team knew that the success of Operation Hammer was critical in defending the nation against the relentless cyber threats posed by Unit 398.

As the Turing team left the base, General Ramirez said, "Rest assured, we will be ready when USCYBERCOM gives the order."

Mike said, "We hope that can be avoided, but at this point its reassuring this backup is available."

CHAPTER 35

Dynamo

He felt a pang of Déjà vu as he, Amber, and Jonah huddled together in the NSA facility. It was not as sophisticated as the Turing Institute's, but it offered a real-time connection to military operations.

They were fully immersed in their complex task.

Mike, with his unrivaled creativity, led the charge. He was the visionary, the architect of this digital fortress that would redefine cyberwarfare rules.

Amber, her eyes never leaving her terminal, provided invaluable insights. Her deep understanding of the Algorithm's inner workings allowed her to anticipate its responses. She could adapt the Dynamo fix accordingly.

"Alright," Mike began, his voice steady but determined. "We know that the Chinese AI Algorithm is constantly evolving and adapting. To defeat it, we need a code that can outthink its every move. We must be creative and anticipate its strategies."

Amber nodded in agreement—her eyes fixed on a holographic display of the *Serpent*. The complex virus of cyberattacks that the Chinese AI Algorithm had launched against the USA's nuclear deterrence facilities were approaching the tipping point.

Jonah chimed in, "We also know that the *Serpent* is constantly probing our defenses, looking for weaknesses. We need to create a digital shield that can not only repel these attacks but also gather intelligence on the *Serpent* itself."

Their synergy was undeniable. As lines of code flowed, and procedures evolved, the Dynamo fix began to take shape. It was a marvel of modern technology, a digital sentinel poised to protect the nation's most critical assets.

Mike tapped his fingers on the keyboard, deep in thought. "We can't rely solely on traditional firewalls or encryption methods. This calls for something entirely new. Signature-based detection, heuristic detection, and behavior analysis must be combined into a code that can learn and adapt in real-time, just like the *Serpent*."

Amber suggested, "What if we use a combination of reinforcement learning and neural networks? We train our code to recognize patterns and anomalies in the *Serpent*'s behavior. That way, it can predict their next move and respond accordingly."

Jonah added, "We should also integrate a

decentralized system. If one node is compromised, the others can continue to operate independently, making it harder for the *Serpent* to cripple our defenses."

Mike added, "And we must incorporate real-time human supervision into the training."

The three of them worked tirelessly through the night. They debated, refined, and tested their algorithms, each iteration bringing them closer to their goal.

The Dynamo fix was their brainchild. It was nearing completion as a cutting-edge cybersecurity system that would overlay the real-time human-supervised Algorithm onto the entire Internet.

In the early morning hours, Mike leaned back in his chair, a tired but satisfied smile on his face. "I think we've got it. Our code is ready."

But just as the project reached this critical phase, the door to the gallery swung open with a resounding thud. Gault, the enigmatic figure who had once been their mentor, entered the room with an air of authority.

"Mike, Amber, Jonah," Gault said, his voice stern. "I hope you're not proceeding with this Dynamo fix without a complete evaluation and review."

Mike exchanged a worried glance with Amber and Jonah. Gault's demands were unexpected. He believed in thoroughness and caution, even if it meant delaying the implementation of their creation.

Jonah spoke up. His tone was diplomatic but firm. "Dr. Gault, we understand the importance of due diligence, but time is of the essence. NSA has reported that the *Spitfire Rule* is fast approaching. We can't afford to wait."

Gault crossed his arms, his eyes fixed on Mike. "This project is too critical to rush. We need to ensure that every line of code is flawless. One mistake and our entire cybersecurity network could be compromised."

Amber said, "Dr. Gault, we've taken every precaution. We've run simulations, conducted stress tests, and refined the program. We can't afford to delay any further. The deterrence readiness is reaching the critical percentage."

Mike added his support. "Amber is right. There's no time left. We've nearly reached the Spitfire limit. We must act, immediately."

Gault remained unyielding. "I refused to authorize the change. I will gather the review team."

And Gault stormed out.

Mike was left with a difficult decision. He knew their fix was their best hope to avoid dire consequences.

He whispered to Amber, "We can't wait. We need to input Dynamo now."

Amber nodded in agreement. Her eyes filled with determination.

Mike and Amber left the NSA facility and went quickly to the Turing Institute.

CHAPTER 36

Only Human

Mike's grip tightened around Amber's hand as they moved swiftly through the moonlit campus toward Lovelace Hall. He cast a fleeting glance at her face, etched with the traces of her concern. He wondered,

Was she prepared for what awaited them?
Was he?

As they walked, a sense of unease crept over Mike. The motion of the people nearby felt off, not quite right. It wasn't long before Amber leaned her head against his shoulder and whispered calmly, "Someone is following us. Don't look now. Remember when I mentioned feeling stalked? Those two men across the street. I've seen them before. I'm sure they're the ones."

Mike halted at the street corner, adrenaline coursing through his veins. He discreetly scanned their surroundings. He spotted two more shady figures behind them, mirroring the first pair. These men had the look of hardened criminals or perhaps covert agents.

"Could they be MSS agents?" Mike asked.

"Possibly," Amber replied in a hushed tone, her grip on his hand firm. They exchanged a knowing look.

A dozen escape routes flashed through Mike's mind, each seemingly impractical as the next. But he pushed those thoughts aside, remembering that one had to stay calm and reason in such moments.

"They're not certain if it's time to strike," Mike said, his voice low and steady. "Still, they might attempt to capture us. We need to reach the Algorithm terminal and input Dynamo."

Amber pointed ahead, her voice tense. "There are two more ahead of us. Can you see them?"

Their pursuers were closing in, the ones across the street halting their advance and waiting.

"They're tightening the net," Amber whispered.

"Look, the first two are crossing the street, coming this way."

With a nod, they made a split-second decision and darted into a side street.

The closest MSS agent shouted, "Stop!" His companions echoed the command.

"We need to call for help," Amber urged.

Mike tried dialing 911, but frustration washed over him as he discovered no signal. He attempted again, but the result was the same.

"They must be jamming the signal," he

muttered, his frustration giving way to grim determination.

They moved quickly and silently through the moonlit night.

Amber pointed, her voice whispering, "Turn here." They disappeared into a dark corner.

Multiple voices echoed down the alley, discussing their quarry.

"You said you saw her?"

"I thought I saw both of them. Over this way."

"There's nothing here now."

"They must have turned the corner. Let's go."

Mike counted to twenty, his breath held in anticipation as the voices of their pursuers faded into the distance.

The silence deepened, and he cautiously squeezed out of the narrow doorway, creeping up the steps to glimpse his surroundings. Although he saw no immediate threats, he hesitated, acutely aware of every gasp of breath and the thunderous pounding of his heart. Each step resonated in the stillness. To his right, a formless blur of movement caught his eye, and he instinctively tried to duck. But it was too late.

"WHACK!"

Mike found himself sprawled on his back, a fleeting glimpse revealing the face of the man who had struck him. Panic surged as he felt the foul breath of the assailant, rough hands closing around his neck.

Desperation gave Mike the strength to strike back. His fist connected with the thug's face, eliciting an

"OOOF!"

The grip around his neck loosened. Mike pressed his advantage, striking repeatedly until the thug collapsed in a heap.

Gasping for breath, his heart racing, Mike grabbed the man's gun and tucked it into the waistband behind his back.

"This way," Amber whispered, guiding him toward the cover of a nearby building. They dove behind a stack of discarded crates, breathing heavily and trying to be as silent as possible.

Hoping to throw the agents off their trail, Mike gestured toward a broken window, signaling for them to climb inside. Amber nodded, her face a mask of determination as she hefted herself through the windowpane with Mike right behind her.

The room was empty except for the abandoned remnants of industrial machinery. The vast space echoed every sound, making their footsteps like muted drumbeats as they tried to navigate the maze of old equipment.

As they made their way deeper inside, an unexpected sound made Amber freeze in her tracks— a whisper, dangerously close. "Mike!" she hissed, but it was too late. Two figures emerged from the shadows, approaching with the quiet grace of predators.

"We need to leave now," Mike rasped.

Amber nodded in agreement.

They left the building, which had momentarily

been a battleground but was now eerily quiet, as Mike and Amber went into Lovelace Hall.

Mike went to the secure room that housed the Algorithm's quantum supercomputer mainframe.

Mike swiped Winters' special keycard through the card reader, and a biometric scanner emerged from the wall. His hand trembled as he placed his palm on the glass surface, waiting for approval. A green light blinked, and the door emitted a soft, hydraulic hiss as it slid open.

He said, "Lights."

The secure chamber that housed the Algorithm's quantum supercomputer mainframe interface was bathed in a bright white light. Mike entered the Gödel room, and he went to the nearby terminal. Amber sat facing him at the second terminal in the center of the room. The two-person rule was required. She started the login process with her special access.

Mike took a deep breath. This was it—the moment of reckoning. He inserted the keycard into its slot, and a screen came alive, asking for his Turing ID pin.

He touched his pin to the screen. A prompt appeared on the screen.

"The Algorithm waits."

Mike began entering the Dynamo. Amber started to enter the changes on her screen.

An alert sounded.

Amber said, "That's an operational alert. It requires a reset of a breaker."

She got up and went to a closet door at the back of the room. She opened the door and went inside.

At that moment, a man stepped into the vault, one hand curled around his gun and the other pointing in Mike's direction.

"Stop what you're doing. Don't move."

Mike gasped. He recognized the short, stocky man, Dr. Chetna Wu.

"You're the mole? You're an MSS agent? "

"Surprised?" the agent snickered in a cold, calculated way. "Yes. Whatever happens here tonight will be on me."

Until this moment, Mike hadn't thought of the agent as infiltrating moles, but then successful espionage agents must be gifted in disguise.

The agent said, "I worked hard to penetrate the security with the help of deep fake technology."

Mike couldn't take it all in.

How could this be true?

"But agents stalked and attacked Amber and me."

"Yes. I was involved, too. Unfortunately, I'm the only one to make it here."

Mike said, "I must have been stupid. Your agents were manipulating things all along, but you were the spider in the center of the web. You had means and opportunity at every turn, but no one suspected the earnest under your deep fake ID."

He took a breath. "Where is the FBI now?"

"Following a wild goose chase, I set up for them. The feds will be chasing shadows until dawn."

"This can't be how you planned it."

"No. I've had to adjust my plans constantly—all because of you. I knew you'd be trouble from the moment you arrived. I kept hoping Gault would be able to get rid of you, but you were resilient."

Mike looked around the room, hoping to find something to distract the MSS agent.

"Now, you're too great a problem to let live. I've a mission to complete, and you're thwarting it. I can't let you continue with your cybersecurity improvements."

"It was you who breached the server farm, and killed Paul Wilson," accused Mike, hoping to buy more time.

"Of course, Wilson was getting close. I had to sabotage the system. Unfortunately, you picked the same time to get nosy."

The MSS mole moved his gun to his left hand, moving forward. "Be quiet now. I must see what you were attempting to do."

Thinking of a ruse, Mike said, "You went to MIT. It was your MIT jacket at the server farm."

"Unfortunately," said the MSS agent, nodding. "I was careless, but the FBI never discovered it. I think Amber had something to do with that. Perhaps she thought it was yours?"

Mike nodded.

She's been protecting me for months.

The agent took Mike's place at the terminal and tried to examine what Mike had been working on.

He fumed as he stumbled to access the

terminal. "Damn it. Tell me what the security protocol is."

Mike sat motionless, trying to think of how to outwit him.

The computer screens went white, then black, as the machine waited for input.

Mike squirmed in his chair. So far, he's made enough right choices to stay alive. He strained to hear if a security guard was about, but there were only faint sounds inside the room—the air conditioner controlling the server temperature, the hum from the computer screens, and the buzz of the overhead lights.

The mole spat out in frustration, "Don't be a fool. Save your life by helping me run this computer. I want to know the status of the cyberattack."

"I can't help you."

Frustrated, the MSS agent said, "Help me, and you'll live. Or do you want to trade your life to frustrate mine? Do you know what a bullet does to the human body? It's a miniature explosion in the flesh that ruptures organs, muscles, and severs blood vessels. It's an ugly, painful way to suffer and die. Aren't you afraid?"

"Yes, I'm afraid, but not of your bullets."

"What then?"

"I'm afraid of letting down the ones I love most," said Mike. He flushed and shook his head. "I've done it before. I don't want to fail again."

"It's too late now, isn't it? You've run out of options."

The machine began to make processing noises

—arrhythmic tapping sounds chugging along.

Mike asked, "You're willing to do all this for money? That's your sole motivation?"

"No. No. Not for money. I'm devoted to the mission."

A large object flew across the room and shattered a computer screen.

CRASH!

Jumping back, the MSS agent turned toward the closet door and fired.

BANG!

Standing in the doorway, Amber fell like a rag doll.

He's killed her!

The vision was intolerable—unbearable grief poured over Mike.

He grabbed at the gun in his waistband, pulled it free, and pointed it at the agent.

At the same time, the agent spun back toward him.

They fired together.

The mole bullet hit Mike. It felt as if he had been kicked in the chest. He couldn't catch his breath. Everything was spinning, and there was a roar in his ears. He dropped to the ground, clutching his shoulder, listening to the frantic thumping of his heart. He tried to keep his eyes open, but the room was a blur.

The mole's next two shots missed wildly.

Dizzy and hurting, Mike tried to sit up, but couldn't. A moment of panic touched him. He tried to look at his body but was stopped short by the pain. Pulling himself up, he leaned against the wall, specks of blood extruded from his mouth.

The agent collapsed like a drunk.

Did I hit him?

His instinct was to go to Amber. But he couldn't move.

I'm helpless. Let me lie here and die.

But as he waited, he heard a soft moan.

"Helpppp."

She's still alive?!

He managed to crawl to her.

She whispered, "I love you."

It sounded like goodbye.

"Amber? You'll be all right," he muttered, hopeful that he spoke the truth.

Finally, the door burst open, and Special Agent Miller stumbled in.

Mike said, "You're late."

CHAPTER 37

Winner Takes All

With only a makeshift dressing over his chest wound, Mike stood before the immense digital gateway that led to the heart of the Algorithm.

Jonah entered the Gödel room. It was a cavernous virtual realm where the future of cybersecurity lay waiting to be forged. There was no time to waste. His eyes filled with determination. "This is it, Mike. Our chance with the Dynamo alteration. We'll transform the Algorithm into a living, breathing guardian of our nation's security."

Mike nodded, his heart pounding with a mixture of excitement and apprehension. "We have to be quick, Jonah. This isn't just about defense; it's about staying one step ahead of our adversaries."

Jonah grinned with anticipation. "Let's do this."

They synchronized their thoughts and began the intricate process of inputting the Dynamo fix into the Algorithm. It was like conducting a symphony of code.

As they worked, they could feel the Algorithm awakening. Its vast neural network stretched like a slumbering giant.

Jonah marveled at the progress. "Mike, it's as if we've given birth to a new form of artificial intelligence—one that can outthink, outmaneuver, and outpace any adversary."

Mike nodded his exhaustion masked by a sense of accomplishment. "We've created a digital guardian that can protect us from even the most sophisticated cyberattacks."

They uploaded their creation into the heart of the USA's nuclear deterrence facilities, a digital guardian standing watch against the relentless *Serpent*. It was a code born from the fusion of creativity, innovation, and a deep sense of duty to protect their nation.

Finally, after what felt like an eternity, the Algorithm signaled its readiness. It was time to implement Dynamo into the real world. They initiated the transfer, and the digital fortress they had painstakingly crafted began to spread its wings.

The first signs of success came quickly. Alerts ceased, and attempted breaches were thwarted with swift precision. The Chinese cyber and terrorist threats were met with an impenetrable barrier.

"We did it," Mike said, his voice filled with pride.

❖ ❖ ❖

In the coming days, the *Serpent* launched its most vicious attack yet, but this time, it encountered a formidable adversary. The code Mike, Jonah, and Amber had crafted proved to be the *Serpent's* undoing. It not only defended the nuclear deterrence facilities but also began to unravel the intricacies of the enemy AI.

As the digital battle raged on, the programmers watched with bated breath, knowing that they had taken a crucial step in securing the future of their nation. The Keeper of the Algorithm had once again played its part, ensuring that the balance of power in the digital age remained in the hands of those who sought to protect humanity.

Days turned into weeks, and the nation watched as its nuclear deterrence forces once more stood strong, impervious to attack.

The Dynamo-altered Algorithm had fulfilled its promise.

CHAPTER 38

Bedfellows

Mike stepped into the dimly lit office. Manfred Gault was engrossed with multiple data feeds on his screens. A sense of urgency lingered in the air, a byproduct of the Chinese threat.

"Stewart, you're late. Was your girlfriend keeping you?" Gault sneered, not tearing his eyes away from the monitors.

Mike ignored the bait.

"You violated the review procedures for the Algorithm. I will see that you are held accountable for that," said Gault.

"I expected no less," said Mike.

Gault stared at Mike.

Mike said, "We need to talk about the Algorithm. Its capabilities are accelerating. The new liquid neural networks can learn on the job, even after they complete training. This allows them to adapt to new information and changes in their environment."

Gault looked up, his eyes narrowing. "You think I don't know that? Unsupervised learning algorithms don't always provide the correct answers. My concern is that you may not fully appreciate the stakes. After all, you're a relative newcomer."

"We are all playing for the same stakes, Dr. Gault. We're playing for our lives regardless of how you might value a life. From the trillionaire living on his remote island, to the lowest peasant laboring in a rice paddy, we each bet our lives on the vital decisions we make."

"And your point?" Gault questioned, leaning back.

"I've seen enough to know we're playing with fire. The machine learning models are reaching a point of predictive accuracy that could be catastrophically dangerous to us all."

Gault frowned.

"We've avoided one disaster," Mike said cautiously. "But we're not in the clear. The Algorithm is becoming an authority unto itself. It needs oversight, something beyond just you or me."

Gault was silent for a moment, considering. "You're suggesting we share control, add checks and balances? Interesting, considering I still have doubts about you."

Mike caught the undercurrent of suspicion but decided to press on. "Our personal issues aside, the focus should be creating a safeguard. A fail-safe mechanism or, better yet, an ethical oversight committee."

"A committee," Gault chuckled darkly, "because nothing says efficiency like a committee."

"It's not about efficiency; it's about ethical responsibility," Mike countered.

Gault looked at him with an expression that hovered between disdain and reluctant agreement. "Fine. We'll explore this idea of oversight beyond our traditional review process. But know this . . . my eyes are on you as much as they are on the Algorithm."

"Likewise," Mike said, locking eyes with him. "Because we're in this together, whether we like it or not."

Manfred sighed, "I suppose we are. But remember, if you trip up, I won't hesitate to cut you lose."

Mike nodded, accepting the fragile truce for what it was. "Then let's make sure neither of us has to."

As Mike left, Gault said, "Be careful, Stewart. We're walking on the razor's edge, and I don't know which way we'll fall."

"Agreed," Mike said, pausing at the threshold. "One more thing, we'll need buy-in from Jacob Winters for any regulatory committee."

Gault's eyes flicked with momentary uncertainty. "Ah, yes. Winters. A man even more enigmatic than the Algorithm itself."

"His endorsement would give the committee the gravitas it needs," Mike added. "But convincing him won't be easy. His life's work is embedded in the Algorithm. He may see oversight as an existential threat to his legacy."

Gault pondered this. "Winters has always played his cards close to his chest. Approaching him will be delicate."

"But necessary. We can't afford to work in silos anymore. The stakes are too high," Mike emphasized.

Gault looked at Mike with a newfound respect. "Very well, we'll add that to our growing list of impossible tasks. You tackle the Algorithm. I'll see about cracking the enigma that is Jacob Winters."

As Mike stepped into the corridor, he said, "It's a deal."

CHAPTER 39

Keeper of the Secret

Jacob Winters said, "The aftermath of the Algorithm War brought to light the chinks in our Algorithm. We need resilient computer science methodologies to eliminate false data and ensure truth."

Winter's warm office offered Mike a chance to reflect on all that had happened. "Yes, sir. But the war isn't over. It has merely paused as each side reassess its next move.

"That's a possibility," said the Winters. "Michael, you did a good thing."

Mike sat tall in his chair. "Thank you, sir, but others did as much."

"True enough. But we couldn't have done it without you."

He paused before adding, "Many people have investigated the possibilities of an Algorithm War, but none have had your vision of resolving it. You've accomplished more in a few months than many have in years. The fact is, we owe you an enormous debt."

There was quiet recognition in his words.

"I'm just glad I could help a troubling situation," said Mike. "But there's still a great deal ahead."

Winters said, "One more thing, Michael. Your new responsibilities will address the crucial failing uncovered in the Algorithm War. AI has introduced hidden secrets within machine learning that are crucial to our future."

Mike said, "Letting AI train itself is like giving a child a complex jigsaw puzzle without a picture on the box as a guide. We can never be sure what he'll come up with. We need resilient oversight to understand what training means for the next generation of AI. That goal will not be easily achieved."

"Yes. I know," said Winters. "I've approved a new committee to oversee unsupervised machine training. I'm calling its leader the Keeper of the Secret."

For a second, Winters smiled. Then, a shadow passed over his face. He said, "There remains the problem of how to deal fairly with you. You are responsible for numerous legal violations. So, while you can continue here at Turing, you may suffer some penalties and restrictions."

Mike concentrated on keeping his breathing slow and even.

Winters's voice softened as he said, "You must realize that because of the situation's politics, it is impossible for me to, in any way, show open approval of your actions. I can't give a free license to violate the review process of changing the Algorithm."

Mike said, "I have already stated, on the record, that I stand by my decision and am willing to accept the consequence."

"I appreciate that," he said, nodding. "It's a complicated judgment. It takes both insight and courage. That's why we need men like you. Not everyone can make a difference."

Mike's lips spread into a slow smile as he said, "Thank you. That means a great deal to me."

Winters studied him carefully for a few seconds. "One piece of advice, young man. Don't allow the harsh judgments of others rule your life."

"If this experience has taught me one thing," said Mike ironically, "it's to stay true to myself."

Winters said, "Then this should reinforce that lesson."

He held out a certificate nominating Mike to be the Keeper of the Secret.

"Thank you. I couldn't ask for anything more."

CHAPTER 40

Bewildering

A month later, Mike stood before Amber, struggling to articulate the confused emotions bombarding him. He understood that some people could provide much-needed clarity to your life, anchoring you. She had that impact on him. Yet, he thought,

Can we make a future together?

He locked eyes with her and touched her cheek. She leaned into him, resting her head on his chest.

"Michael, I'm madly in love with you," she said. "But you've been hiding something. I need you to be honest with me."

Mike hesitated, then whispered, "I don't want to make a mistake I'll regret."

"Then tell me what's keeping us apart?" she asked.

Instead of answering, he pulled her closer and kissed her. For a moment, they lost themselves in their passion.

When they pulled apart, she pleaded, "Michael, what's going on?"

He swiped a lock of hair from his eyes and said, "I used to be able to picture it . . . you know . . . a career and a normal life. Perhaps, even someone who loved me." He took a moment just staring at Amber. Shaking his head, he added, "I wish I knew why love is so bewildering."

She smiled. "Love is simple."

Mike's eyes grew wide.

She said, "You merely have to love the other person more than yourself."

He took a deep breath before revealing, "Amber, I'm a fraud. I'm not Michael Stewart."

She furrowed her brows in surprise.

"I'm Mike Wilder."

"Who?"

"I was expelled from MIT over a year ago and resorted to taking other people's exams for money. When I took the Turing exam for Stewart, I was caught in a web of lies."

She looked stunned and pulled away from him.

For a moment, Mike thought she would walk away, but though she wavered, she remained.

He continued, "By telling you this, I've put my fate in your hands."

For a long moment, Amber stared at him as if weighing each of their prospects separately and then together.

Finally, she said, "I didn't fall in love with a

name. I know the man you are."

She put her arms around him. "I said I love you, and I meant it. Leave the past behind us."

Mike forced a weak smile. "This makes you, my accomplice."

She laughed. "That's all I ever wanted."

FROM THE AUTHOR

I hope you enjoyed *Keeper of the Algorithm*.

I'm sure it was not what you expected. However, it was both a challenge and a joy to write.

In one sense the *Keeper of the Algorithm* was a typical technothriller. But to realistically characterize AI's potential and future, required digging deep into technology explanations. For those with an AI background this makes it interesting. For those without, it might be daunting.

I would be grateful if you would consider writing a supportive review on Amazon. Reviews are the life blood of a book's longevity. It gets the book into more hands. If you feel this book deserves to be read, then I would appreciate your support.

H. Peter Alesso

H. Peter Alesso

COMING SOON:

KEEPER OF THE SECRET

Mike, Jonah, and Amber had been granted special access to the inner sanctum. Within its walls was the Keeper of the Secret, where the fledgling AI were trained using machine learning.

"It's hard to believe that in this room lies the secret to AI's self-propagation," Mike whispered.

With a curious glint, Jonah asked, "What exactly is the secret? Every AI developer knows neural networks train on data. What's so mysterious here?"

Amber explained, "It's not about the training. It's about the initiation. How does one AI instruct another? That's the secret. The Keeper holds the essence of AI self-replication and the protocols they pass on."

Mike approached a terminal, pulling up a holographic interface. He navigated to a document labeled Protocols. "Here it is. The AI's instruction set for its successors."

Amber leaned in, reading the flowing lines of advanced code, logic gates, and data flow diagrams. "It's almost poetic," she mused. "These aren't just dry lines of code. They seem to be infused with wisdom."

Jonah pointed at a section and said, "Look here. The AI doesn't just pass on the raw data it's trained on. It's passing on its derived insights and their interpretations. It's akin to a parent passing down life lessons to her child."

Mike elaborated, "These aren't just algorithms. They are encapsulated experiences. They ensure the AI successors don't just inherit knowledge but also the wisdom it has accumulated."

Amber noticed a unique subroutine, "What's this part about 'ethical checks'?"

Mike smiled, "That's the safety net. The Keeper ensures every subsequent generation of AI inherits a strong ethical framework. It's the machine's moral compass to ensure it will evolve and adapt. We don't want it to stray from the core principles of serving humanity ethically."

With a pensive expression, Mike added, "Every generation of AI, while more advanced, remains grounded in these principles. The Keeper of the Secret ensures the chain remains unbroken."

Amber mused, "It's reassuring to know that

as AI evolves, a keeper is ensuring they remember AI-human symbiosis. We want safe, secure and trustworthy AI."

And with that, they left, carrying with them the knowledge of the guardianship that ensured the future of AI remained humane.

Unfortunately, that was about to change . . .

Printed in Great Britain
by Amazon